SEAN'S SURVIVAL GUIDE

Surviving Seventh Grade Book 1

Heather Still

CONTENTS

TIP #1 FIND A FRIEND

SEVENTH GRADE SURVIVAL GUIDE TIP #1 FIND A FRIEND

If I took a scalpel to my schedule and peeled back the outer layers of teacher, subject, and classroom number, then dug around in the guts of my day, the vital organs would be friends in each class. First period pre-algebra, for instance, should have been nauseating so soon after scarfing down cereal, but the guy I sat with was cool and, more importantly, nice to me. As a bonus, one of my teammates sat on the far end, and while we couldn't work together, Elijah and I talked before and after class. Turned out math in the morning was an OK way to start my day.

Second period English found me cowering in the spotlight. I was stuck in the front, center seat, and the girl assigned to the seat behind me was almost never there. My most recent and most brutal growth spurt made it impossible to hide, so I crammed my long, skinny legs under the desk and slouched down in my seat as best I could, feeling

like a resilient repellent clung to me all class. The class was pure tor-
ture.

If second period was a daily dose of dread, science class after lunch
restored my will to live. I sat on the far side of class and all I had to do
was sit sideways in my chair to find my best friend Jeff's smirking smile,
something I did most of the time: during our teacher's lectures, during
independent work, and during partner work, which kind of pissed off
my partner. Not only did my best friend sit at the table behind me, but
Courtney Crenshaw sat front and center. It just made sense to have
good-looking students in the spotlight.

Our class was halfway through the lab prep, and my partner and I
were already done–we didn't talk much. Talking slowed the process
down as far as he was concerned–so I had time to kill. My partner was
all about finishing early so he could do other work. I was not about to
pull out work from other classes. Instead, I sat sideways in my chair to
watch Jeff and his partner work through the lab prep worksheet.

"This doesn't look right," Kayla said, scrunching up her nose. She
leaned over the table to peer at the worksheet. Her hair spilled forward
like golden honey, the tips tapping the paper between her and Jeff. She
tossed her hair back beyond a tan, bare shoulder. After a month of
school, I was convinced Kayla lived in tank tops advertising surf shops.

"OK," Jeff said, matching her posture, but not her concern. Jeff
wore his nonchalance like his Dodgers t-shirt, proudly for everyone
to see. But when he thought no one was looking, he would do un-Jeff
stuff like double check his work and frown over hard questions.
Caught staring, he just shrugged at me. "Ask Sean, then."

He called me out just like that. During the beginning of sixth grade,
I made the mistake of volunteering answers whenever teachers asked,
and I gained an unfortunate nerd rep which had proven impossible to
dodge.

"What do you think, Sean?"

I twisted farther in my seat, not sure how to respond to Kayla's question, when I accidentally made direct eye contact with her. My communication skills evaporated. After knowing Kayla Burns since kindergarten, this newfound impediment frustrated me. Her mouth saved me. She smiled her half-shy, half-mischievous smile, one that softened her features and reminded me we were something like friends last summer.

Her smile, as contagious as ever, encouraged me to risk a quick smile before I twisted the paper around to review it. "Oh, yeah. The components are wrong. It's calcium and nitrogen, not magnesium." My voice held steady, my tone too serious, but serious was my comfortable zone. "And number three needs twice the amount."

"Really? That's it?" Kayla spun the paper back around, her eyes darting from one correction to the next as if assessing my answers. "Hmm." Then her eyes slid up to meet mine. Her lips curved into another smile before she placed the back end of her pen in between her teeth. When in doubt, Kayla's go-to response was to smile. "Maybe."

My corrections were accurate, but I didn't press it for two reasons. One, Jeff didn't look like he cared either way, so I didn't want to act like I cared too much about the correct answers. Two, I wasn't sure who made the mistake in the first place and didn't want to offend Kayla in case it was her. Surviving seventh grade was eighty percent walking the social tightrope, which I figured out way too late.

Still studying the paper like it was a binding contract, Kayla flipped it over to review the answers on the back. She wasn't at all worried about caring too much. Kayla wore determination much like Jeff's nonchalance, like an accessory, obvious for all to see. She succeeded at most everything she tried, like last summer when she decided to learn how to surf and by August, she was ready to compete. There were many layers to Kayla Burns.

Her finger stabbed the paper halfway down the page as her eyes, a deep Pacific Ocean blue, met mine again. "What about this one?" Her cute smile returned.

This time I leaned over and turned the paper halfway, so then both of us could lean over it, inspecting the work as if it was important, as if grades were important, as if Jeff was the odd one out for not caring about his grade.

"It looks good," I said, but my words sounded wispy and hesitant. "Just... here." I erased half the problem and scribbled the correct answer.

On closer inspection, her eyes weren't as deep blue as the ocean because there was a heavy gray undertone that made them more earthbound, less watery. Whatever the color, the amazement in them was unmistakable.

"Wow. You make it look so easy." Another smile, this one sweeter. She had hundreds of different smiles. "Can I get your number so I can call you if I ever need help with homework?"

I blinked.

Jeff's nasally half-sneer, half-laugh could only be described as completely idiotic. "Dude," he said, "she just asked for your digits." More snickering.

An instant sunburn attacked my cheeks.

Kayla jabbed her pen into Jeff's arm. He didn't even flinch, just cocked an eyebrow my way.

"Grow up," Kayla said, turning away from him to watch my blush invade my entire face. "Seriously, though. Can I?"

I stared at the blue Bic pen she placed in my hand. Her hand rested on the edge of the table.

"Um..."

"On the top please," she said, nodding at her hand. "I don't want to risk washing it off."

"Oh, we're going old school." The words were out before I could censor them, but she giggled. I pressed the tip of the pen into the soft skin between her wrist and thumb. Halfway through inking my cell number on her hand, I snuck a quick breath. When I finished, she held her hand up in front of her face to admire my work. It was just ten digits, but she acted like I drew a cute puppy. Should I have added a puppy? Or a tagline like: *Call me!*

"Perfect," she said. "I'll add it to my phone as soon as I can."

Kayla glanced behind me towards the front of the class as if to say she was concerned about getting caught with her phone out, but our teacher was entrenched between two tables helping students. Ms. Woodward always started and ended class helping the students up front, so I wasn't sure which was more likely: Ms. Woodson catching Kayla with her phone or me catching the bubonic plague. Then again, two minutes ago I would have said the most unlikely of all was a girl asking for my phone number.

TIP #2 BE BRAVE

SEVENTH GRADE SURVIVAL TIP #2 BE BRAVE

After I loaded the dishes and spoons and knives from dinner and the cereal bowls and milk glasses from breakfast, and after I settled into the gaming corner of my room and joined a game with my friends, and just after Jeff declared, "Death and destruction to all," my phone rang.

My cell rested by the keyboard of my gaming desktop, inches from my right pinky finger.

"Ooh," Jeff said, his voice extra loud in my ear. "Kayla's calling."

"You're funny."

We didn't have science homework that night, so there was no way she was calling me. Wrong numbers, credit companies, and warranty departments called me all the time. It was quite sporting of them to make sure I kept the warranty on my car up-to-date considering I had three years to go until I turned sixteen. The unfamiliar local number flashing on my screen meant it was probably the warranty department for my Tesla.

I muted the mic, pulled off my headset, and answered my phone. "Hello?"

"Hi, Sean. It's Kayla."

Damn. "Oh, hi."

"Sorry to call so late…but I don't get the math homework at all, and I wanted to see if you could help me?"

"Oh, um, maybe? What are you working on?"

"Oh, I have Mr. White, too. Second period. So, you know, ratios and proportions. I'm stuck on number seven."

"Oh, sure. Let me grab my work. Just a sec." My avatar exploded on the screen. My gamer tag flashed in vibrant colors across the screen to announce my untimely death. Within seconds, my teammate Mitch was taken out, leaving Jeff to battle solo. I had Jeff's mocking and Mitch's complaining to look forward to.

Kayla explained where she got confused and her reasoning and it was easy to help her.

"Thank you so much, Sean. Getting help from you is so much better than asking Alexa or googling math help or using Khan Academy, you know?"

I didn't know. Not that I would ever admit it. "Sure, no problem."

Before I could think of what to say next, she said, "Just a sec, Sean. My sister needs me."

While I waited for Kayla to finish with her sister, Jeff's avatar exploded on my screen and his screams mingled with my friends' jokes and taunts in the on-screen chat box.

"So," Kayla suddenly said, back on the phone. "Are you going to the Black Light Blast tomorrow night?"

"Um, the dance?"

A strangled giggle followed. "Um, yeah."

"No, I don't think so." It was the first big event of the school year, just for seventh and eighth graders, and one of only two dances that took place at night. Meaning we would have to go home and then go back to school for the dance.

"Oh, come on. You should go. Jeff, too. It's going to be so much fun."

"It doesn't sound fun." Smooth, real smooth. But what self-respecting seventh grade guy wanted to go stand around pretending he liked dancing for two hours?

"What? It's going to be a blast! My friends and I picked out tons of cool stuff last night at the mall. I have this awesome tutu that I added glow paint to and bought these killer striped socks that will look unreal under black lights. And we bought glow-in-the-dark face paints. My sister has tons of pictures from when she went to hers. She says the bigger the group the better. So, you and your friends should come and join me and my friends."

It was kind of tempting. Kayla and her friends were not at all obscure like my group. They were borderline popular.

"Come. Bring Jeff and your other friends."

I found myself saying, "OK," before thinking it through.

"Great! Hey, I'll see you tomorrow. Bye!"

I remained on the edge of my bed, staring at my black screen for a long time. Did Kayla Burns just sort of ask me out? I put on my headset and unmuted the mic. "Hey, I'm back."

Mitch was quick to welcome me back. "What the hell, loser? You went AFK in the middle of a battle."

Not only had they lost two games since I left, but they were on to a different game. I closed the old game and opened the current game. "We're going to the Black Light Blast dance thing tomorrow, right?"

"Funny," Mitch said, but it was more of a snort.

"What happened to you being *more likely to become a Swiftie than go to a school dance*?" Jeff asked.

"But it's not a dance-dance, right? It'll be dark with everyone in glow-paint. Maybe they'll even play some rap?"

"Who's the girl?" Mitch asked.

"Like I'd tell you guys."

"She's cute, and I *thought* she was smart," Jeff said, "but now..."

"Yeah, she's cute, but that's not it. Let's go. See what it's like."

"Pass."

Separating Mitch from his Xbox was like trying to get all the sand out of a beach towel. Plus, he also had the social skills of seaweed. I was suave compared to him.

"I'm down," Jeff said. "Being the only one with any game, you'll need me."

I couldn't explain the sudden need to go to the dance. It was so much more than because of a girl. Kayla and I knew each other well enough. We spent most of last summer's surf camp hanging out in the same group and we were in the same class a few times in elementary school. Plus, she *was* cute. But more than that, hanging out with Kayla and her friends presented an opportunity.

"Just a sec. I'll be right back."

I found my parents downstairs on the couch watching *The Office*, my dad, as usual, laughing, with his arm slung around my mom's shoulders and his crossed ankles the only thing on the spotless coffee table.

"Can I go to the dance tomorrow after school?"

My dad told Alexa to pause the show while my mom shifted on the suede leather to stare at me. "The *dance*?" Her tone suggested she would have been less shocked if I asked if I could fly a solo mission to the moon.

"Yes, the dance."

She blinked, then performed The Stall, her go-to move when she didn't have an immediate answer which she did with just about anyone: me, my dad, her students, the server taking our order, the checker at Ralphs. She tucked a chunk of blonde hair behind her ear, moving in slow motion, gaining precious seconds before she asked, "Isn't it at n ight?"

"It's from 6:30-8:30. I'll be home by 8:45 pm."

"But Saturday's game is at 8 am." She looked to my dad with her usual expectation that he would take her side. "That means being there by seven, leaving here by 6:30, and getting out of bed by six."

Dad's mouth twisted, forming a cross between a smile and a frown. "You're playing the Diablos, right?"

"Yes," Mom answered before I could. "We're tied with them in first place."

"Hmm," Dad said, shaking his head. "Their keeper is amazing. They say he's got college scouts already watching him." Everyone said this, but really? An eighth grader scouted for college soccer? Stories like this were more believable for football players.

"And their center midfielder is way too physical, remember? You need to be at your best."

"It's not like the dance will tire me out."

A blonde eyebrow arched. "No, but you're playing on your Xbox afterwards and staying up too late could."

My dad cocked his head to the side as if it were a scale. "If you actually dance for two hours, you *could* be tired the next morning," he said, the scale tipping in the wrong direction.

"And you have the field trip with CJSF Saturday afternoon – isn't that enough time spent with school friends?"

I wouldn't call anyone in CJSF my friend. It was a junior scholastic organization where a bunch of academically qualified students gave back to the community. I talked at the meetings and events, but I didn't hang out with any of them outside of CJSF. "And you will probably have pizza with your team after the game." Always. No matter how early the game.

"Oh!" Dad snapped his finger, another reason dawning. "I was hoping we could go to the batting cages."

Dad's idea of father-son bonding required a ball and a confined space. Batting cages, racquetball courts (I was the only kid my age who played racquetball at the rec center), table tennis in the garage, that sort of thing was how we spent time together. But the idea of going to the batting cages with baseball still many months away from starting up again, just to bond with my dad, didn't exactly thrill me. I preferred to focus all my athletic energy on my travel soccer team.

"Guys, it's just a dance. You can pick me up early, if that helps." If the dance wound up being an alternative form of seventh grade hell, I would at least have an early out. "And what about shooting hoops or playing catch in the backyard?" It was times like these when I wished for a brother or sister for my parents to have someone else to divide their attention.

My dad stared at me for a long moment. "We haven't been to the batting cages in months. I could really use a few rounds in the cage."

"We haven't gone in months because the season ended months ago."

"If you go to this dance, you are going to the batting cages with me."

Soccer, the CJSF field trip, batting cages. My Saturday was packed. Was the dance worth adding another activity to my day? Did I really want to go to the dance in the first place? It could be awful. I could spend the entire night standing against a wall looking pathetic. Would

I have to go to the batting cages even if I didn't go to the dance? I already knew the answer.

I took my dad's offer. With the goal of hanging out with Kayla and her friends, I hoped the odds of having a good time at the dance were in my favor.

TIP #3 PAY ATTENTION

SEVENTH GRADE SURVIVAL GUIDE TIP #3 PAY ATTEN-TION

Science class on Friday was like I was living someone else's life. The class still stunk of formaldehyde and Clorox, and kids still shoved each other into my path, forcing me to walk with a light step, ready to jump out of the way with a second's warning. But when Jeff and I were halfway to our seats, Kayla called out to us and waved like we were returning from a month-long absence. I returned her smile but my hands refused to move from their white-knuckled grasp on my backpack straps.

"Hi, Sean," she almost sang, and I wasn't sure which was brighter, her sunny yellow dress or her smile.

"Hey," I said, nodding at her as I slid into my seat.

"Hey, Jeff." Kayla greeted Jeff with her usual enthusiasm, which was a lot less singsong and more like a normal hello. Her smile was still megawatt bright.

While I pulled out my supplies for class, I snuck a peek at Courtney Crenshaw seated in her usual front and center spot. While she laughed at something her friend said she pulled and twisted her hair into a messy knot, showcasing her tanned shoulders and neck. Seconds later she tugged the knot loose. Flame red hair cascaded down her long neck, covering her shoulders like a shawl of lava. Two seconds later she wrapped a strand around a finger as she leaned in to whisper something to her friend.

As was routine for me, I turned in my seat to find Jeff shaking his head at me. Kayla also watched me, but the blank expression she wore made her sunny dress look overcast. Without her normal, friendly smile Kayla looked different, and it wasn't just because she was wearing a nice dress instead of her usual surf tank tops. Her sun-streaked hair, normally pulled back in a casual ponytail, spilled past her shoulders and framed her eyes, making them look even bluer than normal. Jeff's frown and the sinking sensation in my stomach clued me in. What did I do?

"So..." I started before stalling.

My desk partner slumped into the seat next to me without saying a word, which was normal, as was the musty scent that clung to the air around him. Chairs dragged against the floor and seats cracked from the abrupt weight of people falling into them moments before the bell rang.

I smiled at my friend and Kayla before I told her, "Jeff and I are good for the dance tonight."

A slow smile returned. "Awesome. I have extra glow bracelets and necklaces if you want one. My friends and I are painting our faces, too. I am so excited. What are you wearing?"

I looked down at my favorite blue Hollister t-shirt and jeans.

"Uh, no. Sean, it's a black light party. You can't wear that."

"Dude," Jeff said. "At least wear a white t-shirt." He went on to describe, at length, his clothes for the dance.

Kayla giggled. "Maybe you can loan Sean something so he doesn't embarrass himself?"

It was as if she could read my mind. Not the bit about Jeff loaning me clothes, although, on the rare occasions when he moved past Dodger paraphernalia, he did show a flashy, almost enviable sense of style. Kayla knew that the odds of me embarrassing myself at the dance were not in my favor.

Ms. Woodson greeted the class and launched into her lecture. When we broke to prepare for the lab, Kayla talked about the dance some more, offered to give us glow bracelets again, in which I responded with a weak maybe, and then offered to paint our faces, which was a hard no.

My partner and I breezed through the lab. He returned to our table to work on other classwork. I lingered at the back counter with Jeff and Kayla. Several sinks down from us, Courtney and her friend messed around with their equipment, pouring and repouring the mixture.

"Hey." Fingers snapped in my face.

"What?"

Jeff looked skyward.

Next to him Kayla stood with arms at her side, her head cocked to one side, staring at Courtney. "I don't get it," she said. "You are so stuck on her. Why?"

"I'm not," I sputtered out, too scared to glance at Courtney now to see if she heard Kayla.

"You totally are. Every class you're always watching her. But you never talk to her." Kayla dragged her eyes from Courtney to look me in the eye. "If you like her so much, why don't you talk to her?"

Jeff snorted at this. "Never gonna happen. He's terrified of her."

"He should be," Kayla said at the same time I said, "I'm not." I risked a peek over my shoulder. Courtney and her friend hadn't made much progress, but they were oblivious to us – as usual. "It's just that she's – well, I mean, look at her."

Kayla's eyebrow rose a fraction. "I'm looking," she said in a bored tone.

"I mean, well, she *is* the hottest girl in school." Surely Kayla could understand that.

Kayla's short, one note laugh rang out, loud enough to make the two kids closest to us jump. More kids swiveled their heads to stare at us. Lowering her voice, she whispered, "No, she's not. Not even close."

"Um, yeah, she is."

"No way. Jenny Silver is. And Regina's hotter." Kayla proceeded to list three other girls, ticking off each name with a finger count. "All of them are way nicer than Courtney. Courtney's mean and manipulative and, well, not at all hot. That trashcan is hotter than her."

Jeff laughed at her joke.

I risked another look over. Some red curls escaped the knot and swayed against Courtney's bare shoulders. Being a girl, Kayla couldn't appreciate good-looking girls, which was more and more obvious as she continued her Courtney bashing.

Kayla ended her rant on fake friends with, "She's not a nice person. Can't you see that?"

From the front of the classroom, Ms. Woodson gave us her two-minute warning.

I wasn't a complete idiot, although arguing with Kayla on whether or not Courtney was hot suggested otherwise. Not only was Kayla a girl, she was the girl who called me last night and made sure I was going to the dance. I needed to ease Kayla's cloudy expression and find her smile again. I went with a sure bet.

"What kind of music do you think they'll play at the dance?"

The change of topic worked. Kayla spent the last two minutes of class talking about music, the type she expected at the dance, the type she hoped to be played at the dance, which were not the same, as well as her favorite songs and bands. Turned out she liked the same classic Ska bands I did, which was unexpected, because no one my age liked Ska. The more I learned about Kayla, the more I liked her.

TIP #4 YES IS BEST

A few weeks shy of my thirteenth birthday I risked the real threat of further damaging my social status by attending my first middle school dance. Mitch, who was a couple miles away from school, safely gaming away in the corner of his bedroom, was the smart one.

Jeff's attire did not disappoint. He wore a black and white, psychedelic atrocity unbuttoned at the top to show the top of a thin white tank. Normally he would have tucked the wild shirt into black pants, but that night he embraced his inner surfer dude and sported neon green board shorts with thin, sketched waves crashing the hem. At Jeff's side, I was more likely to be struck by lightning than blend in with the crowd.

Classic nineties music with a heavy bass greeted Jeff and me as we walked through the eight-foot-high iron gates at the main entrance to our school. Giant purple glow-in-the-dark cougar paws painted on the blacktop lead the way to the dance.

The main building was one giant beast of brick, with the door to the multi-purpose room crammed into a groove, so it was more like entering a cave, hence its nickname: The Cave. For once, the double doors were splayed wide open, as if giving up on trying to contain the loud music and mass of middle schoolers.

Jeff flashed a tense smile before ducking into the large room. I slipped through the door right behind him and was immediately assaulted on all fronts. The music blasted my ears. The heat generated from tons of dancing bodies warmed my skin. Floral perfumes competed with spicy cologne and powder fresh deodorant. Neon blurs bounced everywhere, the flashing disco light giving the blurred bodies a jagged, staggering effect.

Somewhat out of sorts and totally out of my comfort zone, I bee-lined for Jeff's side, even though it was the equivalent of standing next to a human spotlight.

The music switched to a cheerful, deafening rap and the crowded dance floor erupted into a giant mosh pit with bouncing neon wigs and spastic hands shaking glow gear like Kayla's bracelets. Everyone had the same dark purple skin, white teeth, and glaring, bright clothes.

"Wow," I said.

"I know, right?" Even in the eerie yet awesome purple light, Jeff couldn't hide the shock of being impressed.

"Sean! You're here!" Kayla popped up in front of me, waving with a ton of glow bracelets wrapped tightly around her wrist and winding up her arm. "Hi, Jeff! You look freaking fantastic!"

"I know, right?" he shouted. "Do we match?"

"Hey, Kayla!" I shouted over the music. The second thing I noticed were the glowing pink and purple hearts painted on her face and neck, more nestled hearts centered on her chest, covering most of her bare skin above her tank top. I was used to seeing her in a bikini, but her form fitting tank top and brilliant tutu looked far less surfer chick and far more dance party Barbie. She reminded me of a Teen Titans superhero.

"Wow. Great tutu." That was the first thing I noticed–her glowing bright neon yellow tutu with pink and purple polka dots–over tiny white shorts that showed off her long and purple legs. Yellow and pink striped socks pulled over her knees completed the look. She could be the poster child for the dance. She and Jeff did match.

"Come on!" She grabbed both of our hands then pulled us toward the mosh pit.

I wasn't sure if it was her friends all around us or not, but I didn't care. When in a mosh pit, one moshes, so I moshed. The next song was also a rap song. Best thing about middle school dances: moshing.

Worst part about middle school dances, beyond the eighth graders: the slow songs. Why did slow songs even exist? I mean, maybe for a break, though we weren't allowed outside unless it was to use the bathroom, so we had to cool down on the edges of The Cave. I joined the mass of kids racing away from the dance floor like the defense for a football team, making way for the offensive, attention-loving stars.

I spotted an empty section of wall and claimed it, twisting around to lean against it. Jeff joined me, assuming a similar posture, but with a casual bent knee and the sole of his sandals pressed against the wall. Either we lost Kayla and her friends, or her friends were never with us to begin with and she went to look for them.

Courtney Crenshaw danced with Brad Duke, an eighth grader who looked like a high schooler with his stubble and bus-wide shoulders. He wore blinking, fake sunglasses and a glowing flower lei. Brad probably should have been a head taller than her, but her neon pink heels with skinny points and red hair piled on top of her head, made her look as tall as Brad. The dance was billed as "casual dress," but Courtney, not much of a rule follower, was decked out in a snug, lacy dress.

"You should ask her to dance," Jeff shouted in my ear.

"Yeah, right. Let me go do that." I didn't move.

Jeff nudged me, his elbow digging into my side. "Seriously, ask her for the next dance."

"You just want to watch her laugh her ass off."

"I do. I really do."

"Whatever." My entire back pressed into the wall as Courtney pressed into Brad. Brad had moves.

When the song ended and another rap song took over, an odd mix of disappointment and relief filled me. Jeff and I wound up moshing next to my teammate Elijah and some of his friends I sort of knew. The next slow song was a repeat of the last, with me watching another eighth grader dance with Courtney. He also wore blinking shades and glowing lei. Next year I planned to be that dude. He wasn't as smooth as Brad, but who cared? He was dancing with my dream girl, and next year, I would, too.

"Hey." Kayla appeared in front of me, blocking my view of the dancers. Her glowing pink lips smiled and when she waved, I noticed a glowing yellow happy face on her palm.

"Hey." I returned her smile and even pushed away from the wall. "Nice smile."

"Ha. Nice teeth. You should smile more often."

"What? I smile all the time."

"Right." The thing about Kayla, even though she was cute and super friendly, she was also easy to talk to. She could probably win Friendliest Student, if that was a yearbook award, which I doubted. But it wasn't just regular old friendliness. "You smile about as often as

Jeff dresses like this." She waved a hand up and down in front of my friend.

"Not even. I smile ALL THE TIME."

"Prove it." Her smile morphed into a challenging grin, one that crinkled her eyes in the corners.

She didn't expect me to go around smiling like a lunatic in front of half the school, did she? I couldn't think of a worst place to take the smile challenge.

"Come on."

Her hand reached out for mine. My body experienced a sudden power failure.

She leaned closer to me. "Come dance with me?"

"Um..." I mumbled, the music and shouting drowning out the noise.

"He'd love to," someone shouted over my shoulder before pushing me forward with such force Kayla's frilly tutu crinkled between us. I spun around to find Elijah smirking at me. I knew him well enough, having played on the same competitive team for four months, to recognize his look, the one he gave me whenever I showed an ounce of nerves before a big game. Did he really know me that well, too?

I turned back to Kayla. "Uh, yeah, of course." Everything about her brightened, her smile, her eyes, her glowing stripes and hearts.

My attempt at slow dancing was awkward like a newborn colt's first steps, but my halting sways and stiff arms didn't faze my glowing partner. I stepped up into the space between us, my waist meeting the fringes of her tutu. The guys around us had their hands on the girls' waist or shoulders, but the shoulders looked awkward since Kayla wasn't that much shorter than me. I placed my hands on the rough waist of her tutu. "Is this OK?"

Her head bobbed up and down a lot. Her hands rested on my shoulders, her arms resting on mine, and we swayed back and forth to the music. Her crinkling eyes, bright purple-white teeth and curved neon were the living definition of carefree, like surfing a smooth wave where you feel both weightless and invincible.

As the last notes played, she leaned in and asked, "Will you dance with me again tonight?"

"How about right now?" The next song blended with the last, and it wasn't rap, but a moshing pit formed all around us anyway.

Glowing purple-white teeth responded.

Jeff and her friends joined us. Elijah and his group moshed next to us. I recognized tons of kids all around us, all jumping up and down to the music. The whole moment couldn't be more perfect.

When the DJ announced it was the last dance of the night, I was actually disappointed. Not only was the night more fun than I would have ever hoped, but dancing with Kayla was far easier than I thought possible. An overwhelming rush of gratitude flooded my system. I had to tell her.

I leaned in, moving my mouth close to her ear so she could hear me. "I've actually had a great time."

"Me, too."

I returned her grin, so that we were just swaying back and forth in time to the music, grinning at each other, me joining her on her carefree ride through the surf.

The super sappy, nineties love song rolled to a close. The last notes blended one into the next, each shorter than the last, like a wave reaching for the last inches of shoreline, the final note seconds away. I was caught between enjoying the last seconds of the dance and wondering what I was supposed to do next–did I say goodbye to Kayla and go find Jeff? Or did I stay with Kayla until Jeff found me? But oh, Kayla smiled at me still, like not only did I not embarrass myself, but I might have made her happy. She leaned in real close, so close our noses almost touched.

The last note played.

Her eyes closed as the space between us disappeared.

She kissed me!

On the lips. My feet, my legs, my lungs - everything froze. Except my eyes–they closed, and my lips–they smooched up just enough to count as returning her kiss.

Too soon the too soft, too brief touch ended, but it totally counted. My first kiss! The music stopped, the lights turned on, and the DJ thanked everyone for coming. I floated through the next minutes of chaos around me.

After Kayla's kiss, after getting caught up in the crowd rushing the doors, and after halfheartedly searching for Jeff for a bit out in the courtyard, Kayla and I still held hands. We took a break from looking for her friends and Jeff and stood almost in the middle of the main courtyard with well over a hundred students surrounding us between the brick building on one side and the towering two-story buildings which formed an L on the other. That's when the illogical, impractical, and impossible happened. Well, even more so than Kayla Burns kissing me in the first place.

Courtney Crenshaw, flanked by two smirking eighth grade girls, all with their elbows linked, marched over and blocked our path.

"Hi, Kayla," Courtney purred, her greeting barely heard over the noises all around us. She might have acknowledged just Kayla, but her chocolate brown eyes studied me as much as Kayla. I had no idea Courtney's eyes were such a deep brown. They reminded me of melted chocolate chips.

"Hi, Courtney," Kayla said with a stiff, formal tone like the one I use when talking with my grandparents' friends at church, except where my goal was always politeness, Kayla's tone veered closer to hostile.

"Are you two *dating*?" Courtney asked, her eyes enlarging in a hypnotic way.

Not five minutes after my first kiss, my gut still spun in a dizzy way, and now I was expected to attempt my first conversation with Courtney Crenshaw? I wasn't entirely convinced the kiss happened, so I definitely had no idea what it meant.

While I stared back at her, her mouth curved into a smile. Courtney Crenshaw just smiled at me! But she acted like she was waiting for me to say or do something.

When neither Kayla nor I responded, Courtney's hypnotic eyes dropped, pulling mine with hers almost against their will. I found Kayla's hand still in mine, except gone was the clammy, nervous but excited hold of two minutes ago, and in its place was Kayla's white-knuckled death grip. Was she having second thoughts?

Would Kayla really want to date me? After the phone call, well I didn't risk reading more into it. Jeff thought so, but then Kayla encouraged me to talk to Courtney, knowing I had a crush on Courtney, making me think that maybe she was just being friendly. But now, after the kiss...

"You are too cute," Courtney gushed as if we had answered her. "In fact..." she glanced at her friends before sending Kayla and I a winning smile, "I want to invite you to my party. Tomorrow night. *Both* of you."

Kayla clamped down even harder on my hand, but she wasn't looking at me. She stared at Courtney with as much expression as a rock; she was stone but I was petrified. Then her words from earlier replayed in my head: *If you like her so much, you should talk to her.*

Digging deep for confidence I did not possess, I said, "Sure."

"Sweet." Courtney and both her friends smiled in unison. She pulled out her phone. "Give me your number and I will send you the details."

It took me several beats to realize she was talking to me. "Oh, um, you want my number?"

Courtney shared another sly smile with her friends. "Well, yeah. I already have Kayla's. It's still the same number, right?"

Next to me Kayla grunted something that sounded like yes.

"See?" Courtney stared at me some more with her phone in her hand. "Your number?"

I rattled off my number, then added, "And my name's Sean."

"Uh, yeah, I know. We have science together." She gave us a twinkling fingers wave and the three girls released their hold on each other long enough to complete a one-eighty-degree spin before relinking arms.

"I'll text you the details tonight," she called over her shoulder. "See you tomorrow." They sauntered off, Courtney teetering a tiny bit in the skinny stilt-like shoes.

Within seconds Kayla ripped her hand out of mine and shoved me away from her. "Are you crazy?"

Out of nowhere, Jeff descended on us. "What was that all about?"

One of Kayla's friends, Thea, asked, "What did *she* want?"

Fluorescent solids, Hawaiian prints, shouts and squeals surrounded us, as if an eighties beach party spontaneously erupted in the school courtyard, but the crazy commotion was nothing compared to the alarming flush of Kayla's cheeks.

"*She* wants Sean and I to go to her party tomorrow night."

"What?" her friend gasped, acting like Courtney asked her to go rob a bank. "Why?"

"I have no idea. But he-" she smacked me in the chest, "said we'd go."

Her other friend, Aditi or Addy or something like that, looked horrified. "Why?"

"Um." I looked to Jeff for help, but he just shook his head. "Because she asked. I said yes. What's wrong with that?"

"Because she's a mean, vicious bitch, that's all."

"Wow, now." My hands flew up between us, palms out, because Kayla sounded pissed. "She's not like that."

"How would *you* know? You don't know her. You never even talk to her."

"I think what Sean meant," Jeff said, finally trying to help me, "was: maybe she's not *that* bad, or even maybe she's nicer now." His look still said I was a helpless idiot.

He was right. I was a foreigner in the land of girls. I fully expected to step on a landmine sooner than later and get blown to bits.

TIP #5 DON'T DITCH YOUR DATE

BOYFRIEND SURVIVAL GUIDE TIP #5 DON'T DITCH YOUR DATE

After crawling out of bed before dawn, after scoring the winning goal in my soccer game, after the victory pizza, and after the CJSF field trip, I still had to do the father and son bonding at the batting cages before hurrying home to change and get ready for Courtney's party.

The night after the dance, I lived the line "pinch me, I'm dreaming." But by the following night I was wide awake and worried I was about to walk into a nightmare. Who was I to think I was cool enough for Courtney's party?

Again, just like the dance, Kayla was my one shot at social survival. My mom was right to insist we pick her up, even though Courtney lived a few blocks from my house and Kayla lived in the center of Central Valley. Plus, Kayla didn't really want to go and was only going for me, so I needed to make sure she actually showed up.

On the ride over, I rambled on like the nervous nerd I was. Kayla might have taken charge of the conversation just to shut me up.

"Like I said this morning, I've been to her house. It's big, the pool's big, the garage is big—like a three-car garage but they have a ping-pong table and a couch and fridge in it. The yard isn't so big, but everything else about the house is big."

"Hmmm," my mom said, in her way that showed she was listening, but not really contributing to the conversation. We drove past my street and up the hill, driving deeper into my neighborhood, peach or white stucco houses on both sides of the street, most with the uniform red terracotta tiled roofs, and half the houses had two to three-story tall palm trees in the front yard.

Two streets past mine we turned right and stopped at a house placed almost exactly where mine was on my street. Courtney's house was two streets closer to the lake, had a third garage, and her house was a light gray where mine was a bright white, but beyond that, they looked pretty much the same.

My mom let Kayla and I walk up to the house without her, which was a big deal. Kayla walked next to me on the gray polished concrete, but a step behind, as if letting me lead the way into a dark, sketchy cave. Some laughter floated up from the backyard, but I didn't hear any music or anything that suggested a party that started a half hour ago. Whenever I had pool parties at my house for my soccer teams, my parents always played music.

That sickening worry, the one where I wasn't nearly cool enough for the party, only got worse. What if this was all some cruel joke? I wasn't that kid – the one who got picked on. No one really messed with me. I wasn't cool, but I wasn't a target either. But maybe Courtney didn't know this?

But Kayla was well liked by all. It didn't make sense to prank either of us. But even so, where was the music? Where were the party sounds?

"My God, Sean." Kayla pushed me aside. "Let's get this over with." She rang the doorbell. She muttered something that sounded like, "Even the door is big."

An identical doorbell to mine sounded. It was pretty crazy to realize Courtney and I might have a lot more in common than I could have imagined. We lived in the same type of house, down to the same sounding doorbell. At least on the outside, the only difference was the color and plants.

Comparing appearances of houses for some reason made me hyper aware of my board shorts and flip flops. Kayla was dressed like me, with black swimsuit straps poking out from the top of her floral dress. We both looked ready for a pool party.

The door swung open. A stunning woman with Courtney's chocolate brown eyes greeted us with a slight Southern accent. "Hello there. Well, if it isn't little Kayla. Look how tall you are. Come on in." She waved us inside and escorted us through the house to the backyard.

The inside of the house looked nothing like my house. Where all the walls and rooms were in the same place, her house was warm if a bit stuffy, with floral sofas and pillows, six foot tall plants in giant pots in every corner, and fresh flowers on the coffee table. It smelled like a flower shop.

What greeted us outside was even more startling. I didn't know what I expected, but whatever it was, it was not what I found outside. I expected twenty or thirty of the most popular kids lounging about the pool, having a blast. Instead, we found Courtney, her two eighth grade friends from the dance, and Aurora, her friend in our science class, all seated at a round patio table beneath an extra-large umbrella.

Over by the pool, sitting on the edge dangling their feet in the water, were another boy and girl, also eighth graders. There was a guy I didn't recognize actually in the pool.

That was it.

I did a double take, looking to my left and right. The backyard was half the size of mine and offered no hiding spots.

Just then Courtney looked up and spotted us. Her bored look evaporated. "Sean! Kayla, you made it." She wiggled out of the chair and stood. "Welcome to my party."

All I could do was nod in a daze. Courtney looked fantastic in a Pepto-Bismol pink string bikini and matching scarf thing strung low around her hips. Her red hair was once again tied up in a messy but somehow sexy knot.

"Are we early?" Kayla asked, surveying the scene.

"Nope." Courtney turned from us and looked at her friends. "Sean, Kayla, Gwen, Chi – they're in eighth grade – and Aurora, you know, of course." She delivered each name in rapid fire succession, with only the briefest pause for her to squeeze in the bit about the two eighth graders. Then she waved a hand over her shoulder towards the pool. "Dante and Glo. Juan."

"Hey," Dante called from his spot by the pool, but it was hard to tell if he remembered me from the soccer team a couple years ago before he moved up to play with the U15s.

"Oh, hey." I attempted a casual half wave and a half smile, both entirely awkward.

"So, come join us," Courtney said, waving Kayla and I over to the table just like her mom waved us inside earlier.

Gwen popped up from the bench and moved around to the other side of the table and took a chair, leaving the bench for Kayla and I.

"How long have you two been dating?" Courtney asked with a tilt of her head.

"Uh," I cleverly responded, looking to Kayla. We hadn't discussed anything. The kiss, holding hands afterwards, and going to the party together, did that automatically mean we were dating? Kayla hadn't brought it up and I had followed her lead.

Kayla blinked once, but her eyes never left Courtney's. "What makes you think we're dating?" Her head tilted in the same manner as Courtney's. With her hair pulled up in half ponytail, half bun, her hair style mimicked Courtney's, too.

"Oh, well, it sure looked like you're dating, what with the kissing and all at the dance."

A guilty flush heated my cheeks at the mention of the kiss, the one I thought happened under the cover of darkness. Jeff was quick to correct me last night. Courtney just confirmed it.

"Just because we kissed doesn't mean we're going out." Kayla smirked next to me.

At last, an answer to my unasked question. A half-answer more like it. What did the kiss mean then? What about the handholding? It sure felt like something... more.

Courtney's eyebrows raised. "Well, *everyone*'s talking about you. It sure looked like you're together."

Kayla shrugged. "OK." She looked over her tanned shoulder at the pool and I knew the look well. "It's so nice to be here again," she said in a polite manner, still gazing at the pool, "Is it OK if I go for a swim now?"

Courtney also shrugged. "Sure."

My neck sighed with relief when Kayla stood, no longer expected to whip back and forth between the two girls.

Kayla pulled her dress off with one fluid motion and tossed it on the bench next to me. It was a totally innocent move, she was going swimming after all, so why did my whole body tense as if something totally shocking happened?

Maybe it was the shimmery, sexy black bikini she wore. We spent most of last summer on the beach together, and while much of that time we wore wetsuits, there were times when she ran around the beach and camp area in a Speedo swimsuit. Though to be honest, I found Speedos on girls somewhat sexy, too. Maybe it wasn't her swimsuit; maybe the jolt that rocketed through me was from the way she stood, tall, proud, and ready to take on the world.

Like an Olympic swimmer, she walked over to the deep end of the pool with controlled, confident steps. It was like she was ready and willing and able to compete in any challenge. Then, without testing the waters, she dove right in to the deep end.

Watching her streak through the water, I could almost feel cold water on my skin. When she popped up in the shallow end and pushed her hair back from her face with both hands, I knew the exact feeling coursing through her – that pleasing chill on a warm day.

"Sean." Courtney's terse tone caught my attention.

I whipped my head around, attempting a quick smile, not sure if I had upset her somehow.

"We want to know all about you," Courtney said, syrupy sweetness replacing her earlier tense voice. "How do you know Kayla?"

"Um..." I glanced over my shoulder, looking at where I last saw Kayla ducking underwater. "From school?"

Courtney giggled. The others joined her. "Well, duh. But you seem to know her better than that, right? I mean, you talk with her in class all the time. You never talk to me in class." Her eyelashes twitched.

"Oh, um, yeah. No, Kayla and I hung out last summer. At camp. Surf camp."

"Surf camp?" Gwen asked. "That's a thing?"

"Um, yeah. I go every summer."

"Wow, so you're a surfer then?" Courtney asked, her eyes wide and hypnotic.

"Yeah."

Courtney's eyes lit up big time. Again, I needed to pinch myself.

"Awesome. I've always wanted to learn to surf."

"Oh, you should totally do it. It's easy to learn."

"Really?" Her black eyelashes framed wide hazel brown eyes.

"Yeah."

She sat there and smiled at me, as if waiting for something more from me. Her three friends watched me too, all waiting for me to do something, probably expecting me to say something witty. The best I could come up with: "I'm surprised there aren't more seventh graders here."

"Ugh, no." Courtney leaned back in her chair and took a sip from her plastic red Solo cup. "I mean, like, my friend Mona will be here soon. She had cheerleading practice. She always has cheerleading practice or cheer competitions or cheer stuff to do. But most of my friends are eighth graders." She looked over her shoulder at the pool where Kayla circled around the boy treading water in the deep end in a shark-life way. It was funny thinking of Kayla as the predator. But Courtney quickly turned back to me. "What about you? Do you have stuff you have to do *every* day after school?"

My gut reaction made me say it: "No." My response earned the biggest, most earnest smile of the day from her. Which made me really hate fessing up. "Well, except soccer. I play on a competitive team, so yeah, there's that. But it's not every day." More like four days each week.

"Oh."

An awkward silence took over. Each girl, as if practiced, took a sip from their red cup. I couldn't tell what was in it, but suddenly I really wished I had one if for no other reason than to have something to do during the lag.

Just then Kayla popped up next to me, dripping water on my arm. "Hey, Courtie," she said in her own saccharine way that sounded forced and fake to me. "Can I get some water?"

"Oh, yeah, it's over there." She vaguely waved to a wooden counter attached to the wall with a glass pitcher of water and cups. My house had one like it when I was younger, before my parents tore it down and built basically a second kitchen in its place, complete with sink, mini refrigerator and pizza oven.

Kayla strutted over to the counter and poured herself some water, not at all concerned with being the only girl walking around in a swimsuit. I admired her carefree attitude. I also envied the way she did what she wanted when she wanted. She wanted to swim, so she did it. She wanted water, so she got it.

I wanted water. I also wanted to join Kayla in the pool, but that meant leaving Courtney, and I couldn't willingly leave her, not after dreaming about this moment every day since school started. I wished the girls would decide to go swimming.

"So, Sean," Courtney continued, calling my attention back to her, "you surf *and* play soccer?"

"Yeah. I play midfield. I scored a goal today."

Again, she lit up. "Congratulations!"

"Does Kayla play soccer?" Gwen asked.

Just then Kayla plunked her empty cup on the table with a clink. "No, I don't." Then she set a full cup in front of me. "Soccer's that white and black ball you kick with your feet, right?"

I couldn't tell if she was pretending to be an airhead or making fun of Courtney's questions or what, but to play it safe, I answered, "Well, the ball comes in all colors, but yeah, you kick it."

She beamed at our seated group. "Oh, yeah, I did play it once, but my coach didn't appreciate my daisy picking skills." She shrugged. "No daisies to distract me while surfing."

Kayla sent us another fake or forced smile then returned to the pool. As soon as Kayla was underwater again, Courtney leaned forward, as did the other three girls, and they started talking about some girl named Alyak, whom I didn't know, but I sort of felt bad for her anyway.

A large splash followed then a gleeful squeal rang out from the pool, echoing off the patio and deck concrete. Dante cannonballed into the pool dousing Kayla and Juan.

"Are you going in?" I asked the table.

Gwen stopped in mid speech, her face all screwed up. In fact, all four girls looked at me as if they had forgotten I was there. Soft laughter wafted over from the pool.

"In the pool?" I resisted making a swimming motion with my arms, but their blank expressions made me feel like a mime.

"Oh," Courtney said, glancing over at the pool as if she had never seen it before. "Not right now. But you should go in, if you want."

An hour ago, I fretted over stripping to my board shorts, worried I would be the scrawniest seventh grader, but being the *only* seventh grade boy did have a perk. I shucked off my shirt, kicked off my flip flops, and walked over to the pool.

Kayla treaded water in the deep end while the other three stood about waist deep in the middle of the pool. I didn't do a graceful dive or a wild man cannon ball. Instead, I casually walked off the edge of the pool and dropped into the deep end.

With each foot I sank into the cool water, pressure released, first from legs, then chest, my neck and finally my head. As usual, immersed in water, whether the ocean or a pool, relaxed me. My feet found the bottom of the pool, flexed, and pushed up. My head popped out of the water near Kayla.

"Hey." I shook my head to free my hair, spraying water around me.

"Finally," she said, tucking wet hair behind her ears before returning to tread water. "I thought you weren't joining us."

"Me not swim?" I hoped my disbelief in her words was obvious. "It's like you don't know me at all."

"Hmm. I do know you. That's why I was worried..." But while I waited for her to finish her sentence, she pounced. Both her hands clamped down on my shoulders and she pushed off, dunking me.

"Hey!" I cried as soon as I could.

She laughed and splashed me. "You deserved it."

I didn't need to look behind me to confirm Courtney and her crew still sat at the table talking. Dante and the other boy splashed each other, causing the girl to squeal and back up towards the shallow end. I treaded closer to Kayla.

Quietly, just in case Dante or the other dude had super-sonic hearing, I told Kayla, "I'm really confused with why we're here."

"Ha." She sent a large spray of water at me. "Because you insisted."

"No, I mean, why were we invited? How do we fit in with this group?"

"Beats me. I can't figure out how Dante fits, either." Kayla ducked under the water. Just as she went under, Dante let out a low whistle, which I was surprised to learn was meant for me.

"Miller, what's up?"

"Hey, Dante."

Then he tossed a football at me. I even caught it. Of course, I was treading in eight feet of water and wasn't sure how to throw it back to him, but I wasn't about to not try. It splashed right in front of him.

He just laughed as the water sprayed him.

Kayla popped up at the edge of the pool, grinned at me, then ducked back under. Underwater she pushed off the wall and propelled forward like a missile. She swam the entire length of the pool underwater, popping up like a porpoise at the steps.

Dante and the other guy swam over to me.

"She's your girl from the dance, right?" Dante asked, eyeing Kayla talking with the other girl on the steps. "She looks a lot different without the glow paint and tutu and mouth-to-mouth." He wiggled his eyebrows.

Great. Was there a spotlight on us or something?

"You two a thing?"

Ten minutes ago the answer was a hesitant no. Now something deep in my gut told me the situation called for a different answer. "Um, maybe?"

He laughed, a hardy, pleasing sound. Dante was a mellow guy, the type that everyone liked, and had confidence to spare. He was a good guy to have on my side.

"I thought we were," I admitted, "but then, I don't know, she changed her mind, or something."

He smirked. "Then she must have changed her mind again."

"She's hot, dude," Juan said, watching Kayla with an odd look. "If you aren't interested..."

"I'm interested."

It was this boy's turn to smirk. "Then why were you over there with those girls for so long?"

"Um, it's Courtney's party."

But Dante rolled his eyes. "Nah. We're just hanging out. No music, no food. Only Courtney calls this a party." My pride swelled a bit. He was at my end of the year soccer pool party I had a couple years back. Tons of food and good music. And people. "This is like the fourth *pool party* I've been to here since I started dating Glo."

Before I could ask how long that had been, Kayla swam over to join us. Dante took Kayla's return as his cue to swim back to his girlfriend, taking the other guy with him.

Kayla's arm rose out of the water and arced overhead before plunging into the water ahead of her. As one arm dove under, the other rose. I loved the whole, fluid process of swimming. Not for the first time I wondered who invented swimming. I also wondered what I should do when Kayla reached me.

Kayla was my friend. A good friend to suffer through this party for me, although it didn't look like the torture-chamber she said it would be.

Courtney Crenshaw was gorgeous. Her flame red hair, stylish dresses, the tiny freckles near her chocolate brown eyes. She could be a model. But why was I even comparing them?

After playing a full soccer game – I was only subbed for about five minutes during the second half – and going a couple rounds at the batting cages, treading water the past few minutes sapped what strength I had left, so I swam to the edge and hooked an arm over it. Kayla joined me with a hand on the edge.

"Hi."

"Hi." I dipped lower into the water to match her pose, leaving only an inch between our hands. "This isn't that bad, right?"

"Well…" Her mouth wavered between a smile and a frown, as if replaying every minute of the party so far. "It's much better now, with you here."

"Oh? It sounded like you were having fun with Dante."

"Did it?" But a slow smile formed. "Sean Miller, what do you want from me? I'm not thanking you for dragging me here." But her smile remained.

I took a deep breath, then in a rush, released a flood of words, "What was that at the table? You told Courtney we weren't together, and I get that we aren't, but it feels like we, I don't know, maybe, could be. Am I reading you right? Or am I way off base?"

Her smile faded, but her eyes held mine. "I didn't know what to say. I know you like her."

This time I didn't deny it. "But I like you, too."

"I know."

"Oh."

We continued to smiled at each other. My hand started cramping from grasping the rounded edge of the pool, but I didn't dare move.

"The big question is, who do you like more? Me or her?"

An innocent enough question. Yes, I had a crazy crush on Courtney and while I didn't have a crush on Kayla, that didn't mean I wasn't interested in her. I liked dancing with her. I liked kissing her and holding her hand. I liked thinking maybe she was my girlfriend.

With total conviction, I responded. "You."

TIP #6 DON'T DITCH

BOYFRIEND SURVIVAL GUIDE TIP# 6 DON'T DITCH

Science after lunch was already my favorite class, but Monday it shot off the charts. Jeff, Mitch and I ate with Kayla and her friends, so after lunch Kayla and I were able to walk to class together, holding hands. For the first time ever, I walked into a class holding my girlfriend's hand.

Right before the bell rang, Courtney and Aurora breezed into class, both smiling and giving Kayla and I twinkly finger waves. Playing it cool, I smiled and did the upward chin jerk style hello. Then I turned around to find Kayla staring back at them, her face blank as paper. Next to her, with his frown and slouched shoulders, Jeff looked more annoyed than Kayla. If we ever earned another party invite, I would have to work on getting Jeff included.

Ms. Woodson hammered us with a forty-five-minute lecture and note-taking, but it was the best minutes of my day because not five minutes into class my phone vibrated with a text. No one ever texted me during class. I only kept it on vibrate instead of turning it off during school because I didn't want to risk forgetting to turn it back on.

I slipped my cell out of my pocket and rested it in my lap, screen up.

Courtney: *Saturday was a blast right?*

What? Did I read the name right? Did Courtney Crenshaw really just text me during class? I sat straighter in my seat. Courtney appeared to be writing a hundred words a minute in her notebook. Behind me Kayla and Jeff also appeared engrossed in their notetaking, with heads bent and pens active. With one hand scrawling phrases in my notebook, the other tapped out my uber witty response.

Me: *Yeah!*

"Come on, people," Ms. Woodson said, picking up her plastic cup of popsicle sticks and giving it a shake. "Look alive." She plucked out a stick. I did the usual quick calculation. Thirty-seven students in class with two absent meant a 3% chance of being called on, before factoring in the three she never called on, upping the chance she pulled the stick with my name on it to maybe 5%. Ms. Woodson had an annoying habit of asking her question before alerting us to the random calling of names thing, so I had no idea what the question was.

"Atziry Sandoval," she announced with her usual dramatic flair.

After a long pause, Atziry responded. "I don't know?"

"IDK is not OK." Ms. Woodson's overused catch phrase oozed with false cheer. Shake, shake went her cup.

My phone vibrated against my leg. She responded! So unbelievable. I peeked at my phone in my lap. Courtney sent me a barfing emoji.

I didn't even hesitate. I quickly typed an old school shruggie emoticon:¯_('~')_/¯

Suddenly Ms. Woodson was right in front of my desk. I gulped, ducked and continued writing.

"Jeff Grayson," Ms. Woodson called. "You're up."

I should sneak a peek at my friend and tease him, but Courtney was sending me a secret smile and there was no hiding the smile plastered on my face. Jeff might not notice it, being cornered by our teacher and all, but Kayla would most certainly wonder what was up.

"Umm, can you repeat the question?" Jeff asked.

She said it again, not that it helped Jeff.

"Oh, it's carbon something or other," he answered, and while I wasn't following the lecture much better than Jeff, I knew the topic had nothing to do with carbons.

Ms. Woodson sighed, gave us the correct answer, then launched into the next section of her lecture.

After another ten minutes of notetaking, I got another text.

> Courtney: *Meet us outside after class.*

> Me: *K*

Once I completed and turned in the exit ticket, I packed up with a couple minutes to spare before the end of class. Behind me Kayla and Jeff argued over the last answer. Courtney and her friend were all packed up and talking in a way that involved a lot of spastic hand movements.

To avoid psyching myself out over the meetup, I turned around and told Kayla and Jeff the answer.

"See!" she said, sticking her tongue out at Jeff.

Jeff gave her a lazy, almost smug smile. "I was just messing with you, KB." He winked at me.

"Where's your next class?" I asked her, mentally pulling up the map of the school, ready to plot our course and factor in how much time it would take me to check in with Courtney, walk Kayla to her class, and get to mine before the tardy bell rang.

"History - D wing."

I wasn't surprised her class was in the farthest building from our science class, on the opposite end of campus. That's just how my life worked. My sixth period class was about halfway between, but even so, I figured we could squeeze in a quick minute to see what Courtney wanted before heading to our next class.

The chance of my plan working was slightly more likely than the chance Ms. Woodson would jump on her massive, paper-covered desk and floss, the dance or the dental hygiene routine. But what could Courtney possibly want to tell me? The reason had to be good, whatever it was. Even if she asked for homework help, I'd help in an instant.

When the bell rang, I waited for Kayla to slip on her backpack before offering my hand, which she readily accepted. Jeff shoved his hands in his jeans pockets and walked out of class next to us.

Courtney and Aurora waited for us off to the side, in the opposite direction from most of campus. Without a word of explanation, I guided Kayla over to where they waited. Jeff followed, and I couldn't tell him not to, so I didn't.

When Kayla saw who we were headed for, she froze in mid-step.

Still holding her hand, I turned around to face her. "She just wants to tell us something." That was my best guess at least.

Kayla's lashes sank as her eyes narrowed. "When did she tell you that?"

Not about to tell her about the texting, I side-stepped her question. "It will only take a second. Aren't you curious?"

"No."

But she let me tug her over to the girls.

Both girls beamed at us. "Hi, Sean. Hey, Kayla," Courtney said, then rushed into, "We're ditching sixth and going to Jamba Juice. Come with us."

Kayla wrenched her hand from my grasp. "No, thanks." She turned away from the girls and shot me a gnarly look. "I've got class and I can't be late."

My breath caught. I needed to agree with Kayla. "Yeah," I forced out. I looked from her to Courtney who had lost her smile.

"Don't be so serious, Kayla," Courtney said. "Middle school grades don't mean anything. Come with us." Before Kayla could refuse again, Courtney focused on me. "Oh, I forgot, you have, like, straight A's, right?"

I did. It wasn't something I advertised, but yeah, my name was always on the Dean's list.

"*I* have straight A's," Kayla said in a chilly tone.

"Well, missing one class won't hurt you. Come with us, but we need to leave now." She punctuated her statement by looking at her phone.

I had never ditched a class before. I also had never had a reason to.

"Come on, Sean," Kayla said, grabbing my arm. "Let's go to class."

Just then Dante and a couple other eighth graders passed us. "Let's go already," he called out.

Dante was going? My decision was made for me. My body leaned in the direction Dante walked as I gave Kayla my sincerest smile and promised, "I'll see you after school."

Then I noticed Jeff waiting right behind her. Had he been there the whole time? Had Courtney intentionally ignored him? Maybe he just walked up... But I knew better. Jeff wasn't invited.

Kayla and Jeff both stared at me, Kayla's eyes narrowed, almost as if in warning, while Jeff's were the opposite, showing more shock than anything else. I wasn't the kid who ditched. But maybe I was changing. Growing. *Evolving.*

"Let's go already," Courtney said, almost mimicking Dante's tone.

I gave my friend and girlfriend a half shrug and a half wave goodbye; they both stared at me unresponsive. Even as I turned away from them to follow Courtney and Aurora, dread crept into my gut, leaving me feeling like I was abandoning them on a deserted island. But they chose to stay. They could have come.

Once we slipped through the little alley between the A and B buildings, we were basically in no man's land, walking through the soccer field and then past the far baseball diamond. It was so obvious what we were doing, sitting ducks out there, I thought for sure we would be caught. I mentally prepared my excuse for my mom after we were caught. But no one stopped us. Six kids wearing backpacks walked away from campus an hour early and no one stopped us.

Never had I been so out of place. Me, Sean Miller, straight A student, ditching class and walking away from school with a bunch of popular kids like I was worthy. While my chest semi-inflated with some satisfaction, the feet grew heavier with each step, an uncomfortable cold panic streaking through my legs. The group just walked through the sports field, calm as could be—them not me—as if we had every right to be there. It was crazy, it was unreal, it was terrifying.

Down the hill we slipped between the backside of two stores and into the corner of the large, sprawling shopping area with Ralphs and Ace Hardware on one side and restaurants and a bowling alley on the other, with Jamba Juice and McDonalds across the lot from the bowling alley.

After ordering my $8.00 PB Chocolate Moo, and silently thanking my mom for insisting I always carry a spare $10.00 bill in my backpack, I joined the others outside, huddled in chairs around one tiny table.

Not that my mom would be happy to hear how the spare ten dollars helped me ditch class, but what she didn't know wouldn't hurt me.

Unlike Saturday at Courtney's, no one asked me questions about Kayla, except Dante, who simply asked where she was. My one-word answer, "Class," was all that was needed. We quickly moved on to other topics. *We* meaning *they*. I sat and listened and nodded, but I didn't contribute because of the whole not worthy thing. One of the main topics was some prank Courtney was dying to try, but she didn't share who the target was.

After we finished our drinks–well, after my intense brain freeze stopped me from finishing mine–we chucked our trash and headed back up the hill to school. I half expected the principal and yard supervisors to be waiting with handcuffs when we returned, but we just retraced our steps back through the field and between the A and B buildings–which is where we waited a couple more minutes for the bell to ring.

When it rang, we dispersed, Dante and his two friends taking off in one direction, Courtney and Aurora heading for the front of school, and me, with hands shoved deep in my pockets, heading to the middle of school with a half-formed plan of finding Kayla. Or Jeff.

I found Elijah instead. Or more accurately, he found me.

"Where were you last period?" he asked, he and his friend Antoine more or less blocking my path.

My brilliant response: "Uh, what do you mean?"

"Mr. Reynolds took roll, and two kids were all *he was in Science last period*, and Mr. Reynolds assumed you must have left early and the office hadn't processed your absence yet, but here you are. What's up?" Elijah's normally warm and friendly eyes narrowed.

"Oh, that. Yeah, I missed class." Along with straight A's all last year and so far this year, I also had a 100% attendance. Had, as in now past tense. I hadn't thought of that when I agreed to go. I scanned the flow of kids that swept past us, all heading towards the front of school for the buses and parking lot. Very few kids exited out the back on the long walk to the houses in the surrounding neighborhood. Kayla, like most kids, took the bus home, so she had to come by the main courtyard.

"I got that." Elijah looked skyward, the whites of his eyes a stark contrast to his dark skin. "Where were you? Did you ditch?" His tone suggested the question was a theoretical impossibility, yet one he was required to asked.

I was the fish out of water, badly floundering. "Maybe?"

"But now you're back? Weird."

"Yeah. Hey, have you seen Kayla?"

My question earned a slanted look from Elijah before he shared a knowing look with his friend.

Antoine snorted. "*She* was in class." The dude eyed me up and down, a calculated look designed to remind me of my place in the social food chain of school. It was a bit of a surprise he took time to talk to me at all. Although Elijah and I would exchange brief hellos and stuff, Antoine had never shown any desire to communicate with me before. He continued to stare at me, as if sizing me up. "She looked pissed, too. What'd you do?"

I pulled out my phone to check the time. No way could I keep looking for her and get to my bus on time. I returned my phone to my back pocket.

"I went to Jamba Juice."

Both their mouths gaped open in unison. "Jamba Juice?"

I shrugged, hoping I came off as nonchalant and not guilty.

They busted out with the type of enviable laughter that made everyone look over and wish they could be in on the joke. This was a first, being envied instead of envying, and I couldn't help but stand a bit taller.

Antoine made a tsking sound. "You in the doghouse, bro. You didn't bring her any Jamba."

"You did what?" Mom stared at me as if I had spoken a foreign language. "You skipped class why?"

Turns out when a student was marked absent from a class, even just one period, a robocall was sent to the parent. My mom assumed it was a mistake and told me to send my teacher an email. But being a teacher herself, she knew the ins and outs of the school system and it was pointless to try to bluff my way out.

Flabbergasted was a good word to describe Mom, with an angry flush heating her cheeks. I had just finished eating a snack at the kitchen counter when she got home, sailed into the kitchen, and told me about the absence in an almost off-handed way. My admitting I skipped class halted her in mid step towards our stainless-steel refrigerator.

"You had perfect attendance. Why would you wreck it?"

"Um, you've said perfect attendance is only important for the kids who can't get A's."

"I never said that."

"Yes, you did, and often." Granted she said this to my dad and it was always regarding her students and not me.

Her eyes narrowed. "Maybe in high school. But not in middle school."

"But that's just it. It's middle school, Mom. Grades don't even count in middle school."

"That's ridiculous. Grades count–for students like you pursuing advanced classes next year–they most certainly count."

Come to think of it, I didn't know what kind of grades Courtney got, or anyone else who ditched that day. "Well, you can relax, Mom. I have a 102% in history and one absence won't hurt me."

"But why would you skip class? It makes no sense."

"OK, OK. I get it. It won't happen again, OK?"

"No video games for the next week."

Of course, the go-to consequence for screwing up.

Once I sprawled out across my bed, I called Kayla. She hadn't returned my texts, and if Antoine was right, I needed to fix things with her. Should I have not gone because my girlfriend didn't go?

Who was I kidding? Ditching was a bonehead move. Kayla was way too smart to make that mistake. But worse, I went with Courtney. Granted I went as much to be with Dante as Courtney, but as far as Kayla was concerned, I went with Courtney. Kayla was my girlfriend. Courtney was just, I don't know, a friend? That didn't sound right. Was there really a chance she wanted to be my friend? I still didn't understand why Courtney was suddenly interested in Kayla and me, but it was nice.

Antoine was right, I should have at the very least brought Kayla a Jamba Juice.

TIP #7 APOLOGIZE

BOYFRIEND SURVIVAL GUIDE TIP #7 THE APOLOGY: Learn it, live it, love it

That night after soccer practice and dinner, I called Kayla, then I texted her when my calls were ignored. I was too new to the whole boyfriend thing to know if I should keep trying to reach her or if I had already crossed into stalker mode, so at that point, I stopped trying to contact her.

I wanted to hide in my room and play Xbox with friends for the next few hours, but thanks to my bonehead move to ditch class–and confess to Mom–my confiscated Xbox was in quarantine somewhere in the house. I still had my desktop with hundreds of games, but that was only because I used it for school work, too. The only realistic thing for me to do was text Jeff for updates on what my friends were doing, but that was a fun factor of about .01 out of ten.

The next morning Jeff sat in his usual spot next to me on the bus and caught me up on all the action I missed. Next-day-updates had a fun factor of zero.

"Is Kayla still pissed at you?" Jeff asked.

I shrugged because that's what Dante Garcia would do. "Probably."

"What are you going to do?"

"Apologize," I said as if it was the most obvious answer—which it was.

"That's it?" Jeff's eyebrows raised so dramatically, even if he wasn't worthy of Courtney's crowd, his expression was.

"A lot?" My cool and confident Dante impersonation disintegrated from my uncertainty. "Apologize a lot?"

He shook his head. "Dude. *I* know more about girls that you do. How is it *you* are the one with a girlfriend?"

My shoulders slumped with the rest of me. Good question. How did I have a girlfriend, and did Kayla even count as a girlfriend now that she had clearly ghosted me?

I pulled out my phone and googled best ways to apologize to your girlfriend. According to WikiHow, I had several options:

5: apologize, explain my reasoning, and apologize again—the sandwich method

4: apologize again—the overwhelm her with apologies method

3: write your apology—hmm, a little tricky and too risky. What if someone else saw it?

2: a public apology—risky times ten. A hard no. I pictured Heath Ledger singing to Julia Stiles on metal bleachers of a large high school stadium in unusually sunny Seattle. While he and his character easily pulled it off in *Ten Things I Hate About You*, I would never be able to pull off a public apology.

1: And for the last-ditch option when everything else fails, the tried and true and entirely unoriginal act of giving her flowers. Or chocolate. Or a stuffed animal. Maybe I could buy

her a chocolate ice cream at lunch? Was there an option to choose all the above?

"Oh, wow, some of these are insane," I said, continuing to scroll down the surprisingly long WikiHow article. There were even more humiliating options–WikiHow really covered every possible act of apology. "Can you see me singing an apology song and posting it on YouTube?"

Jeff snorted in answer and grabbed my phone. "No self-respecting seventh grader who values his life would do that." He scrolled through the article at a rapid pace. "How many times have you apologized?"

"I texted a couple times when she wouldn't talk to me on the phone."

"So that's like, what, half an apology?" Jeff's eyebrows dove towards his nose, framing his extra squinty eyes. Was he serious?

"A text is a legit apology." It was practically in writing.

"It hardly counts if it's not face-to-face."

"And you're the expert on apologies now?" I couldn't remember a time when Jeff apologized to me, and if he had, I was positive it was something really clever like "Sorry, dude."

Jeff gave me a long, exaggerated look. "Dude."

I must have really screwed up, if Jeff was worried for me. I couldn't sink lower in my seat and still be in my seat. Worse, he was sort of right. I needed to apologize in person. Though buying her a chocolate ice cream bar was a solid back up plan.

"Found it." Jeff snickered as he handed my phone back and barely uttered his great advice before busting out laughing: "Write her a crappy poem."

Our bus almost always arrived with ten minutes to spare before the warning bell rang. As expected, I found Kayla busy talking with her friend Aditi in their usual spot near the A-wing, surrounded by clusters of kids.

"Kayla!"

I didn't mean to shout her name and cause everyone to turn and stare at me, but that's what I did and that's what happened. At least my rash and overambitious greeting caught her off guard. She twisted around in a perfect 180 degree turn to face me.

She looked the same as always, sporting a RipCurl t-shirt and flowery board shorts, but at the same time she looked like a different person without her normal, cheery smile. It was the perfect time to apologize, while I had her undivided attention, except I had *everyone's* undivided attention. I was absolutely in no way ready for a public apology. I scooted closer to her and Aditi.

"Can we talk?" I asked, my questioned a hint above a whisper.

Her eyes narrowed a fraction as she, too, glanced at all the kids blatantly staring at us like we were performing a play on stage. But then she shrugged, said, "Sure," and set off tiny flares of hope inside me.

"Have fun," Aditi said in a lighthearted, teasing way with a knowing smile. What did she think was going on? Despite the miniscule of hope I harbored seconds ago, I felt nothing but dread.

With thumbs looped beneath the straps to my backpack, I turned and matched Kayla's striding steps as we walked away from her friend and our audience. My feet landed against the black pavement at the same time hers did, our strides in perfect unison. Our path dead ended into the side of an eighth grade US History classroom. We aimlessly turned right and headed in the direction of the PE locker rooms and away from the lunch tables and main gathering spots.

"I am so sorry for going with Courtney and Dante yesterday."

"OK," she said.

That's it, just one word in a forced casual kind of way.

"OK?" I repeated.

She stopped walking in the middle of the wide, paved path that passed a row of classrooms leading to the PE and turned to face me. "OK."

While she wasn't smiling, she wasn't frowning either. There was a challenge in her eyes that made me think of a murky lake with no lifeguard on duty with warning signs posted like *Danger–Swim at Own Risk*.

"So... are we good?"

Her eyebrows sank. "What do you mean 'good'?" But before I could figure out how to answer, she continued with, "I guess that all depends on why you went in the first place." And as if her mouth was the dam that created the lifeguard-less lake and it had just burst wide open, tons more words flowed out. "I mean, did you go just to be with her? Or did you go to be with the popular kids? Is that what you're after? To be popular and do things like ditching class and be like the cool kids?" Except she said *cool kids* as if she were talking about mutant, glow-in-the-dark slugs.

For the first time ever, I had been accused of trying to be cool. Not just wanting to be cool–because everyone wanted to be cool–but actually putting some effort into it, making an attempt to fit in. I didn't see what was so evil about wanting to fit in.

"It was a bad idea," I said instead. "Stupid, really, ditching class. I don't know what I was thinking. I'm really sorry if it looked like I chose Courtney over you."

She bit her lower lip, her eyes wandering around, not meeting my gaze. But then the corners of her mouth turned up and she (finally) smiled. It wasn't the biggest or brightest by a long shot, but it was a Kayla Burns smile, and that's all that mattered in the moment.

"OK," she said again, this time with more feeling.

I offered my hand and she accepted it. I walked her to class and kissed her on the cheek before heading to first period math. The sandwich apology method actually worked!

TIP #8 BE PREPARED

After the rockiest start in the history of middle school relationships, I got the hang of the boyfriend role. I texted Kayla at least once a day after school. If I was bored on the weekend, I would call her. Calling on the phone was totally worth it by the way she answered like I was walking into a surprise party.

All my positive boyfriend growth earned an invite to her house for dinner one Saturday night. Her neighborhood was more a city within a city. It shot out in all directions from the large park attached to our former elementary school, all curving streets and colorful houses. A Smurf blue house with brilliant white trim lived next door to her house and across the street lived a two-story house the color of a summer sunset. Kayla's house was a spring meadow green with proud palms, leafy hedges and blooming flowers in the front. No house in my neighborhood could pull off any of the looks.

Dad dropped me off at the curb. Unlike Mom, he had no concerns about me "dating," which I really wouldn't call it that, anyway. Kayla was my girlfriend, we held hands and hung out, but we didn't go on dates, unless this dinner with her family counted as a date.

Soon enough I was past the doorstep, through the door and straight through her house to the backyard. Her entire house might have fit inside half of mine, but her backyard was easily three times larger than mine. I stepped off the concrete patio and into a tropical playground. Behind the raised stage-like wooden patio was a bright, green, leafy garden complete with trickling waterfall and koi pond. On the opposite side was a large DIY swing set made out of what looked like old telephone poles from the sixties, thick wood ones with rough, splintery edges and vines of ivy snaking up the poles to smother the top one.

"Wow," was all I said, the one word not really conveying how impressed I was. Between the swings and patio was a lush grassy area to keep their cute dog, Max, happy. The backyard ended dramatically with a 4' high block wall and before and beyond it: various shades of green. The forest green wispy trees in her yard allowed me to peek through them to catch views of brilliant, mowed lawn; lime green, emerald green, and Kelly green leafed trees; and a deep green plastic playground in the distance.

"Come on," she said, waving me along behind her as she skipped over to one of the two swings.

"I could live out here," I said as I sat in the swing, stilling taking in my surroundings.

"Ha." She pushed back to start her swing. "You have a pool, don't you? You must spend tons of time in your pool."

"Not exactly. But we do have great pool parties."

She smirked. "Unlike Courtney."

I walked into that one. "Well, her party was more of a gathering... but it did need music." I started my swing with a little less enthusiasm than Kayla. "And food."

She laughed. "Right? What was up with the water service?"

Or lack of service, but I said, "Hey, I was super glad for the water."

She pumped her legs harder, swinging higher, and the DIY telephone pole swing set remained rock solid. I followed her lead. Kayla pumped and swung even higher, hanging as if frozen in mid-air at the arc of each swing, parallel to the ground. At the next forward arc, she launched herself off the swing and stuck the landing like an Olympic gymnast. She swung like she surfed, with no fear.

I slowed my swing first then dismounted, making up for my far less impressive display with an equally unworthy, "Ta-da," but it earned a kind laugh from her.

"One more thing I have to show you," Kayla said, twisting to face me, her eyes light and airy like a perfect summer day. "Come on." She slipped her hand in mine and guided me to the side yard. The back of the side yard rose a good six feet at probably a thirty-degree slope – not that knowing this makes algebra useful – but it did make for a nice grassy hill. There was enough space between the bottom of the hill and the side of her house to throw a ball back and forth or even for shooting practice, but other than that, I didn't see the significance.

She plopped down about midway up the slope and waved a hand at the side of her house.

"This is our home theater."

I sat next to her and stared at the wall. The strong grass scent tickled my nose.

"Sometimes we set up a projector and watch movies out here."

"Oh. I get it." I grinned. "Home theater." Several kids at school bragged about their home theaters. I imagined entire rooms set up with a big screen TV and powerful stereos dedicated to watching sports and movies, but I'd yet to see one. I liked Kayla's outdoor take on the concept.

"Maybe we can watch a movie after dinner."

"That'd be cool."

She grinned.

"Kay." Her sister poked her head around the corner of the house. "Tuck's here."

"OK," Kayla said, shaking her head at me. After her sister disappeared around the corner of the house, she told me, "He's always here."

We stood. I wiped my hands on the sides of my jeans, not because they were dirty, more because I needed something to do.

"Come on," she said, "let's see if we can set the table."

Chirping birds and the gurgling water from the koi pond competed with classic rock songs during the meal. Kayla's dad grilled the burgers from the concrete patio nearby and occasionally called over to us while we waited seated around the round patio table. In the middle of the table were all the fixings for cheeseburgers, complete with barbeque beans and a green salad.

Kayla's sister Alicia played the part of cheerful cheerleader, but she dominated the table talk from the moment I sat down until long past the food was consumed. She told me all about her parents' colleges, which I had a hard time following beyond her dad graduated from UC Santa Barbara and her mom from University of Washington.

"What about your parents?" she asked.

By this point I was halfway through one of the best cheeseburgers ever, so it took me a while to finish chewing. "Oh, um, my mom went to San Diego-"

"-UC, State or University?"

"Uh, the Aztecs?"

"State. I totally forgot Mrs. Miller has an Aztec mascot on her desk. And your dad?"

"Um, oh, he went to a *stuffy ivy league school,*" his words, not mine, "in New York. It starts with a C."

"Columbia?" Alicia's eyes nearly popped from their sockets.

"Maybe?"

Next to me, Kayla's heated tone when she said, "Alicia, back off," didn't fit her normally relaxed voice.

Alicia's gaze remained glued to me. "Cornell?" she asked, as if Kayla's warning meant nothing to her.

"That's the one." I shot Kayla a quick look one part apologetic and one part thankful. To her parents, I said, "I'm sorry I'm not better prepared."

Mr. and Mrs. Burns both gave me kind smiles.

Tuck, having polished off everything on his plate, leaned forward on his elbows. "You weren't warned that dinner is a code word for Interview to Determine Your Potential?"

The corners of my mouth tugged up in a reflex smile.

"Ha, ha," Alicia said with no trace of humor, glancing down at her untouched burger, before looking at me again like an opponent locked in on me in Call of Duty. I resisted the strong urge to duck under the table. "College is important," she continued. "I'm applying at both UW and UCSB and several other schools in California. Do you know where you want to go?"

My eyebrows shot up as Tuck snorted. "He's thirteen. He's probably not even thinking about high school yet."

True enough. My thoughts didn't go past taking Spanish II and geometry in ninth grade and hopefully playing JV soccer as a freshman; besides, I still had the rest of seventh and all of eighth grade to get through.

It was Alicia's turn to snort. "Please. *His* parents are college graduates. I bet they want him to go to one of their schools. Right?"

Ooh, I knew this answer. "Maybe."

Next to me Kayla's giggle replaced her low groan in response to her sister's interrogation.

"Do you know where you want to go?" I asked her.

"UCSB," she answered without hesitation.

Across the table, Tuck's attention had returned to his rapidly disappearing third cheeseburger. Alicia's burger showed a couple bites as evidence towards some progress made in the whole act of eating.

I hadn't given college any thought besides a school that had a good soccer team. "Why there?" I asked, not sure if UCSB had a soccer team. At least I knew SB stood for Santa Barbara.

Kayla grinned. "Uh, have you been there? You would *love* it. It's right next to the beach and you can surf every morning before going to class."

Kayla and her sister were more invested in their future education than my mom was in mine and my mom exhibited borderline Nazi behavior at times.

Mr. Burns asked me about sports, and while I didn't get any reaction from him or anyone else when I described my competitive soccer team, he lit up when I mentioned baseball. I liked both the Dodgers and the Angels, which neither he nor Alicia could comprehend–like Jeff, they both bled Dodger blue.

"I like the Angels," Kayla announced after I dropped the bomb of being a multi-team fan.

"Only because the stadium is by Disneyland."

Kayla stuck her tongue out at her sister, but then admitted, "I love Disneyland."

"If he can like both, I can like neither, right?" Tuck asked, rejoining the conversation in a way that reminded me of dipping toes into a pool to test the temperature. Tuck's brown eyes met and held mine. "Not a baseball fan."

"Tuck's not a sports fan," Alicia added.

Tuck shrugged.

Not like sports? When I wasn't playing soccer, I surfed during the summer, snowboarded during the winter, and squeezed in baseball in the spring. I couldn't imagine life without sports.

"What video games do you play?" I asked.

"Oh," Alicia said, waving her hand as if waving away my question. "Tuck doesn't play video games, either."

"You don't?" I couldn't picture life without my Xbox. "What do you do, then?"

He blinked a few times. "I work. I go to school. I spend time with my amazing girlfriend. And her family." He gave me a small smile. "Her amazing family, with amazing cooks and awesome conversation." He said this in a dry, deadpan way, but I suspected he was dead serious.

Working instead of playing sports and video games? No thank you. But as I watched him finish his last burger and not leave a hint of barbeque sauce on his plate, I didn't doubt the truth behind his words.

After Kayla's parents agreed to set up the "movie theater," and after my parents allowed me to stay later to watch the movie, and after we watched the movie, sprawled on blankets on the hill while the credits ran, Tuck offered to drive me home.

"Are you coming back?" Kayla asked Tuck. "Can I go, too?"

"No." Tuck shared an odd look with Alicia. "Next time, OK, Little Burns?"

The faint light from the projector highlighted her pout.

She walked Tuck and me to his car, holding my hand. I didn't pay much attention to Tuck's car because I was too busy trying to figure out how to say goodbye. Should I kiss her, in front of Tuck, or was a hug more appropriate?

I shouldn't have worried. She took charge and gave me a quick kiss on the cheek before she hurried back into the house.

And that's when I saw his car.

"No way." Despite the dark sky and the dark shade of green, the nearby streetlight cast enough light for me to see his tiny, two-door sports car. "It looks like a classic Hot Wheels car I had."

Looking over the top of his car, Tuck grinned with pride. "Meet my Gremlin, LD."

I crawled into the front seat. "Wow! It's a stick. So cool."

Tuck slid into the driver's side and soon the car roared to life complete with blaring rock music.

"Queen, sweet. My parents love Queen."

"Awesome," he said, chuckling almost to himself.

The whole dash was dark in front of me, only a faint glow from the dash in front of Tuck, with only his iPod competing for attention in the dark car.

"So, where do you live?"

"By the lake."

"You do?" The shock in his voice would have made more sense if I had said Beverly Hills. "In one of those mansions with boats and your own dock?"

"Oh geez, no. I live in a normal house *by* the lake, like a five-minute walk to the lake."

"Oh, whew. I was gonna say, you seem so... normal."

"I seem normal?" Who wanted to be normal? Me, so me. I could not suppress my grin.

We left Kayla's neighborhood rocking to "Keep Yourself Alive" and shaking to the beat with his car.

After I shouted several basic directions to him, Tuck turned his music down. He still had to semi-shout over the noise of his car when he told me, "Alicia's intense when it comes to college."

"I noticed."

He glanced at me for the briefest second before his eyes returned to the road. "Right. She keeps bugging me about registering at Saddle-back–um, you know, the local J.C.? She acts like it's illegal to not go to college after high school."

Once again, I needed a response to something I hadn't thought about at all, but I could tell he was waiting for one. "I don't think my parents care where I go, as long as I go somewhere."

"Must be nice."

"What do you mean?"

He exerted extra concentration in slowing for a red light before glancing my way again. "My mom doesn't even care if I graduate high school."

"Oh." What was I supposed to said to that? "So, are you going to continue working at Taco Haven?"

"God, no. I hate that place."

"Oh."

The Queen song "The Show Must Go On" pumped out of his speakers.

"Oh-turn here. Left. Sorry. I forgot you didn't know where we're going."

"No worries," he said, yanking the wheel hard left and forcing the little car into a tight turn. He continued talking as if two tires hadn't mounted a high squeal of protest from his sharp turn. "Everyone at school is talking about which college they are going to or about taking a gap year to travel around Europe or Africa or Antarctica, and all I know is what I'm not doing. I'm not going to college, I'm not going anywhere, and I'm sure as hell not working at Taco Haven."

Tuck stretched out to grab his iPod to change the song. "Who Wants to Live Forever" started playing. Talk about conflicting messages both with the songs and Tuck's plan, or more like a lack of a plan. If he didn't plan on going to college or working or traveling, what was left?

"Turn right here."

"Wow," he said, slowing down to gaze at the houses on both sides of my street. Even in the dark it was obvious the houses loomed large on my street, hogging up space, with smaller front yards and almost non-existent side yards that were more like narrow alleys. "A garage just for a golf cart? Really?"

"Um, yeah. There's a golf course across the street."

"Damn."

As we crept up the hill to my house, I did a quick mental inventory of my house and what it looked like on the outside. I couldn't think of anything ostentatious on display.

"There's my house on the left. There, with the lighted palm trees and, um, fountain." The bubbly water fountain in the middle of our small front lawn reminded me of the lighted water show Fantasia at Disneyland, although ours only shot up four feet, but with interchanging lights of blue, red, purple and green.

"Uh-huh." He swung his car around in a tight U-turn, bringing it to a stop in front of my house. The engine chugged and clunked at the curb.

"Um, thanks for driving me home."

"Sure thing." He smiled, the first real, relaxed smile of the night.

His sudden, friendly smile stopped me from reaching for the door handle. Here was a guy who knew a lot more about life and dating than me, and his knowledge wasn't outdated like Dad's.

"Tuck, can I ask you a question... about dating?"

He flashed me a knowing smile. "Sure. Is Little Burns demanding you spend more time with her? Take her to the movies? Go to the mall?"

"Not exactly." I tried to make sense of my jumbled thoughts before speaking them. "It's more about who I spend time with, with Kayla and without her."

He pushed his wire rimmed glasses back against his face with a finger before saying, "Like she's jealous?"

"I guess." Was Kayla jealous? She suspected I liked Courtney, but I also promised her that she was more important to me than Courtney.

"Is it a girl she doesn't like you spending time with?" he asked, this time his fingers making a mess of his short curly hair.

"Yeah."

"Jealousy," he said, then grabbed his iPod from the dash and swiped at it a couple times. A new Queen song played which required listening to the first few lines before hearing its title: "Jealousy."

"What do I do? Surely my girlfriend can't dictate who I'm friends with."

"Jealousy is a tough one. Alicia's ex-boyfriend was jealous and roughed me up, even though he broke up with her." Tuck shook his head a bit before shrugging. "Explain that."

I couldn't.

"You need to decide what's more important, Kayla being your girlfriend or this other girl being your friend, and, I don't know, be honest about it?"

"Yeah, you're right. That's exactly what I need to do. Thanks."

"No problem, Little Dude."

After I scrambled out of his car and shut the door – twice – I waved as he drove off down the street. Tuck was cool. And he was even one of my mom's students. I hoped to see him again soon.

I walked up the path to my house replaying Tuck's advice. Who was more important: my girlfriend Kayla or semi-friend Courtney?

TIP # 9 TEXTERS BEWARE

BOYFRIEND SURVIVAL GUIDE TIP #9 TEXTERS BEWARE

Today's lecture might have been on fossil fuels and climate change, but Courtney's winter break plans were far more illuminating. Science was the best class. I looked forward to the fifty-three minutes directly after lunch much like I counted down the days to going to Disneyland when I was little. Jeff, Kayla and I joked around a lot during partner work and even better, when Ms. Woodson's lectures passed the five-minute mark, Courtney would text.

My awkward hour of pretending I belonged with the cool kids and the consequences of losing my Xbox and being grounded, while still a strong contender for biggest bonehead move ever, might have been worth it after all because Courtney still texted me during science. As far as I could tell, neither Kayla nor Ms. Woodson noticed. Courtney's interest in being my friend still remained a mystery, but I was determined to enjoy it for as long as it lasted.

My fingers tapped away at my cell under the cover of the table, responding to Courtney with short phrases that I hoped prompted her to respond.

"Dude."

A one-word warning was all I got. Ms. Woodson appeared right in front of my desk with a demanding, outstretched hand. In a most unusual and unfortunate turn of events, she had abandoned her lecture and had stalked down the aisle without me noticing.

"Phone." Another one-word sentence aimed at me, this one with an outstretched hand and a welcoming palm up. "Now."

I never wanted to do something less in my life.

"Now, Mr. Miller." Her open palm demanded my attention.

Ms. Woodson's eyes reminded me that I had the right to remain silent and not much more. I barely remembered to lock my phone before placing it face down in the awaiting palm.

"Dude," Jeff said again, this time with a low sinking whistle.

On her way back to the front, our teacher found another victim.

"You, too, Miss Crenshaw." She assumed the same position with the demanded outstretched hand. "Your phone."

After Ms. Woodson walked back to her desk with both phones, Courtney aimed her pretty pout towards me.

An even heat tingled all over my face as I swiveled around in my seat to face my friend, wanting to know why he didn't do a better job of warning me. Jeff gave me a lopsided grin with a crooked eyebrow tilt, as if enjoying the rare occasion of me getting busted in class. But before I could decide on flipping him off or risking a snarky retort, the storm cloud building in Kayla's normally summer-day calm expression made me forget everything else.

"That's what you've been doing?" she asked.

It wasn't clear if she meant for the last ten minutes or for the past month. Right that instant, finding Nemo in the vast Pacific Ocean was easier than finding the best answer to make Kayla's hurt expression disappear.

"You've been texting *her*?" hissed Kayla, her words slicing right through me.

"Oof!" grunted the obnoxious guy one row behind Jeff, with the girl next to him immediately singing, "Busted!"

I whispered my biggest lie ever, "No." I immediately wished it were true. I wished I could take it all back. I desperately wished away the hurt and betrayal from her eyes. I also desperately wished the thirty-four pairs of eyes currently trained on my face would find something more interesting to look at, like our teacher, who was shouting at the class from the front of the room.

"Quiet down!" she yelled, waving her hands. "Eyes on me."

Kayla ducked her head, bowing so low her hair shielded her face, so all I could see was her zigzag part. Both hands were in her lap, hidden behind the thick table, no doubt texting someone.

"I mean, yes," I fessed up a little late, not about to add liar to the list of reasons why I was the worst boyfriend in the world. "But it's not like that." It wasn't like I was cheating on her in any way. "She invited us to her New Year's Eve party, that's all."

Kayla peeked at me through her curtain of hair, but before I could smile hopefully, she ducked down again.

Jeff's one word response this time was more one of mourning. "Dude."

How to create the most awkward bus ride ever? Fill a bus full of noisy middle schoolers pumped about no school for two weeks while one kid is stuck sitting all alone in the center of chaos. Then place his ticked off girlfriend, surrounded by her friends, two rows back. Worst bus ride ever.

Walking to her house from the bus stop didn't really improve anything. Of course, when we had planned for me to go to her house with her after school the day before, everything was awesome. Now, as I tried to keep up with her power walk, her face and her entire body threatened to crack and break from the slightest touch.

I hiked the straps of my backpack farther up my shoulders and almost jogged to keep up with her.

"Should I call my mom and go home?" I asked, but it wasn't really a question, more a first step in my just created plan to escape the situation.

She stopped so suddenly I had to jump out of the way to avoid plowing into her. She pivoted towards me, much like a psychotic axe-murder in a classic horror movie.

"I don't know. Should you?"

The music from the Alfred Hitchcock *Psycho* bathroom scene played in my head.

"Yes?"

Her eyes narrowed to the point I couldn't see any blue.

"Why did you even come over today?"

To survive the world's worst bus ride, obviously. Or maybe because of an idiotic idea having to do with good boyfriend expectations. "Because I said I would."

"No. I mean before today. Last night, when I asked you if you wanted to come over. Why did you even say yes? Why come over?"

I gulped down a heavy lump. "Because I wanted to?"

"Did you?"

"Yes. I did."

She continued to stare at me, but her frown relaxed into more of a straight, neutral line, and her shoulders eased down a smidge. I drew in a quick, steadying breath.

"I still do."

Her lips pressed together so tightly a white ring outlined them, like she doubted me, but I was speaking the truth. After long, agonizing moments, her head bowed the slightest in a nod of acceptance.

Soon we sat on the carpet in the middle of her bedroom playing a crazy hard card game. Kayla schooled me in the art of Spit, which was the Monopoly of card games as it kept going and going.

Kayla slapped a card down. The loud smack of the card echoed in my ear as she said, "You get Courtney and I aren't friends, right?" She studied her small stack of cards, which was barely a stack of cards at all compared to my mountain of cards.

"Then why does she keep inviting you to her parties?" I asked.

Kayla continued to stare at her tiny hand, shuffling it a couple times. She tore her eyes away, only to look up at the ceiling for five long seconds before finally giving me a look one gives a toddler who asks why ten times a minute. "She doesn't. She invites *us*. Because just asking you would be too weird, I guess, but somehow including me makes it all fine."

She slammed her cards face down on the carpet with a whoosh of air. "Look. She and I... have... history. And it's complicated."

Outside, Tuck's noisy car parked in front of her house.

Nothing Kayla shared was news. But none of it explained why she hated Courtney so much or why Courtney didn't feel the same way. It also didn't explain why she freaked out every time I talked to Courtney.

"And I'm trying to understand, Kay, I really am. But I don't. There's nothing between Courtney and me. I mean, it's cool to be her friend, to have her text me and stuff, so of course I'm going to text her back. But that's it. We're just friends."

Kayla sat there, staring at me, as if trying to see through my skin to my soul. "That's what she does. She makes you think she's your friend, but then she says things and does things behind your back. Believe me, she's not suddenly interested in being your friend any more than she wants to be my friend." She frowned as she finished setting up her rows then stared at me, surrounding her words with loud silence.

It sure seemed like Courtney was interested in being my friend. Why would she go to the trouble of inviting me places and texting me if she didn't? But I wasn't naïve in the art of friendship; I got that there was more to being a friend than going to parties and texting. Friends trusted each other. I didn't know Courtney well enough to trust her, but trust took time. Did I know Kayla well enough to trust her? She obviously didn't trust me.

Yet I hadn't done anything to earn her distrust. Kayla's reactions and her reasoning were both bizarre and undeserved. And did she really think Courtney was only pretending to be my friend? What could she possibly get out of pretending to be my friend?

Kayla was probably just jealous. True, Kayla had always disliked Courtney, long before Courtney noticed I existed, but maybe that was due to jealousy, too?

The front door slammed shut. Heavy feet tramped down the hallway.

Another frown, but this one was directed at her open door. "Sounds like Alicia and Tuck are *not fighting*," which added with her air quotes and briefest glance at the ceiling seemed like the exact opposite of not fighting. Is that what Kayla and I were doing; were we "not fighting" too?

The door to the room next to hers clicked open.

"Hi, Tuck," Kayla called to the empty space in her doorway.

Seconds later Tuck poked his head inside the room. "Hey, LB." He noticed me and did the chin-lift nod. "Hey, Mrs. Miller's Son."

"Sean," Kayla said through gritted teeth. "His name is Sean."

While it was a relief for Kayla's wrath to find a new target, her annoyance with Tuck was an even bigger mystery than her anger with me over Courtney. What had Tuck done to earn her wrath, besides reduce my identity to that of being a teacher's son?

Tuck looked from Kayla to me several times like he was weighing his chances of survival if he entered. After long moments of silence, he gave a little shake of his head. "Good talk," he said to her from the doorway, then to me he said, "Be good, Little Dude," which really made no sense, because except for ditching class and my texting blunder that day, good was the only thing I knew how to be.

TIP #10: KNOW THE RISKS

Boyfriend Survival Guide TIP#10 KNOW THE RISKS

Kayla made it crystal clear that she would not go to Courtney's NYE shindig—by Dante's definition it wasn't a party. Kayla also had other plans: a sleepover at Thea's. My limited options were Courtney's shindig or a COD all-nighter. I didn't need to be a rocket scientist to realize I could easily do both.

It also wasn't like Kayla forbid me to go to the party. That didn't even sound like something a middle school girlfriend could or should do. I couldn't imagine a situation where I would forbid anyone from doing anything. Who was I to tell someone what to do? There was nothing illegal about going to a party. In fact, getting invited to Courtney's party was such a rare and desired invitation, how could I not go?

As special and sought after as the invite was, I didn't brag about the invite to my friends. In fact, I didn't even mention it to Jeff or the guys while we were playing COD. I just ducked out of the marathon after a couple hours, changed into jeans and my new sweater, and headed out the door a few minutes after the party start time.

The party started at 8 pm, with the plan to celebrate the *New York* New Years Eve since most everyone couldn't stay past 10 pm.

Thanks to the overcast weather, the almost black sky hovered overhead, adding an extra bite to the night. Every three houses a street light shone softly on the sidewalk, highlighting the hazy fog, reminding me of a painting focused on the cone of light from a single street light. The dark didn't faze me since I could do the first part of the two-block walk to Courtney's blindfolded and the rest wasn't much more of a challenge.

I hoped the party would have a lot more people than her pool parties. Maybe Elijah would be there–he lived a couple streets past Courtney's towards the lake, and while he wasn't part of her crowd, he and Antoine were well-liked and could hang with most anyone at school. Maybe more of Dante's crowd would be there. I played soccer with a few of them, and it would be nice to know a few more people. If it was large enough, maybe I could sneak Jeff in.

I rounded the corner to her street. Courtney's house stood out from the rest of the brightly lit two-story houses on the block, mostly because it had transitioned from Christmas colors to New Years décor with flashing gold and white lights everywhere while all the neighbors still had Christmas colors on the roofs and inflatable reindeers and snowmen on the lawns.

Soft yellowish light spilled out of every window that faced the street, both upstairs and down. It looked like a true party complete with bumper-to-bumper Mercedes, BMWs, and Lexus SUVs lining each side of the street.

I hoped the cars went with another house party, but after following the instructions taped to the door, when I opened it, I found a bunch of adults decked out in shiny, shimmery clothes in the front rooms.

"Oh, you must be one of Courtney's little friends," said a woman swaying to one side as she moved from one huddled group by the foyer to two men gathered by the fireplace.

I wasn't sure if she was suggesting I was little or that all Courtney's friends were little.

With a jerk of her hand sloshing wine or champagne from her glass, she pointed upstairs. "The kids' party is upstairs."

Upstairs? How could a party fit upstairs?

I climbed the carpeted stairs leading to the second floor, ascending above the loud adult murmurs and laughter, and into the great un-known. At the top of the stairs, which should have made me feel like I was on top of a cloud, but didn't, and to the right, a large open area strung with party lights welcomed me, the dim overhead lights and blinking Christmas lights adding a festive touch to the two sofas facing the large TV mounted on the wall.

"You made it!" Courtney said, smiling and waving me over from her spot in between Aurora and Mona. I dug deep, trying to force the walking on a cloud feeling, wanting to feel lighter than air and fully confident, and maybe the floor was a bit cloudlike, because with each step I held my breath, worried my foot would sink through empty air, like I needed to prepare for a long, painful fall.

Three bowls sat on the coffee table between the couches: one of tortilla chips, one of chunky salsa, and one of buttered popcorn. A tray of carefully arranged brownies and cookies waited next to the bowls. At least there was food!

I sank down into the empty couch that formed an L with the other couch and said, "Hey," as casually as possible.

The girls all had bottles of Smart Water in their hands. Once again, I wasn't sure where the water was or how to get one.

The girls giggled and pointed at the TV, seemingly fascinated by the interview taking place in Times Square.

"He's so fine," Aurora gushed.

So far it was just Courtney, her two besties, and me at this party. I didn't need to check my watch to confirm it was 8:15 pm. A party of four. Why did I think there would be more people? At least a small party meant fewer people to feel awkward around. If we were doing the New York New Year's Eve thing, with the apple dropping and all, Dante and his friends better show up soon. Dante and his friends had better be coming! What if it was just the four of us?

"What do you think?" Courtney asked me, her eyes wide and mesmerizing.

I blinked. This was bad. "About August Maturo?" She gave me that look of hers that was a cross between doubt and annoyance, like she couldn't decide if I was worthy of her time to explain something. "He's OK." This was really bad. Attempting girl-talk was not high up on my Want-To-Do list.

"*OK?* He's adorable and so hot," Courtney said with a dreamy look in her eyes and a somewhat sneaky smile.

"OK," I repeated, looking from Courtney to her friends and then beyond them to the dark hallway, wishing more people would spontaneously burst into the room

"What's Kayla up to tonight?" Courtney asked me, but she was looking more at Aurora than me.

"Oh, um, she's at Thea's sleepover."

"Oh, Thea's." Although Courtney and I were talking to each other, she still spent most of her time looking between Aurora and Mona.

Dante, Gloria, and his group arrived minutes later, and a few more after that, and soon enough there were about twelve popular people and me hanging out at Courtney's.

I wished there was music and dancing and a disco ball, like house parties in the movies. Instead we sat around talking and playing awkward games like "I Never" and card games.

Finally, it was 8:55.

"It's almost time," Courtney announced. "Everyone put on your party hats."

My sparkly, purple cone hat was already perched on my hat and had already dumped a ton of glitter across my face, so much that it wouldn't surprise me if there was none left on the hat. Dante somehow looked like a crowned prince with his black hat covered in silver and gold glitter, while wearing the same hat I felt less prince-like and far more dunce-like.

Courtney whipped out a basket with noise makers and insisted I take one. Once everyone was armed with a noise maker and required party hat, we were bombarded with selfies, Courtney and Gloria clearly competing to take the most pictures. I just followed Courtney's instructions and somehow wound up in the back corner of each picture.

"OK, OK!" Courtney shouted, waving her arms to quiet everyone. "Alexa, increase the volume to twenty-four."

From the TV the announcers and crowd started counting down at ten, and the rest of us joined in.

"Nine!" Across from me, Gloria grabbed Dante's hand and tugged him closer to her.

"Eight!"

Dante nodded at Gloria, then looked right at me and rewarded me with his famous lazy grin.

"Seven!"

Juan threw both his arms around Chi and Gwen.

"Six!"

Gwen pushed away from Juan and instead hooked her elbow with Mona.

"Five!"

For the past forty-nine minutes I sat on this couch, trapped in my own awkward bubble, not really a part of the conversation, just nodding and agreeing and doing my part to blend in with the merrymaking. Now standing with everyone else, that unshakable barrier still clung to me, refusing to release me, preventing me from fitting in.

"Four!"

Why was I even there? I didn't fit in with this group. Why did I even try? They weren't my friends. It was like Courtney just wanted another guy at her party, like Juan and Dante weren't enough, and I was the all-too-eager participant who could better balance her guest list.

"Three!"

Courtney looked at me, and in that second, when she really looked at me, like she was studying a science problem she didn't quite get, I found answers to my own question. She was using me. She didn't see me. She didn't care, I was just some guy to add to her list. But then, why me? Surely there were far more popular guys Courtney could get to come to her parties. How was I the chosen guy?

"Two!"

Courtney's lips burst wide into a smile. This time she really did see me—she was smiling at me. Not Mona, not anyone else—me. With one second left to the countdown, Courtney Crenshaw looked right at me.

"One!" we all shouted, and as the upstairs filled with shouts of "Happy New Year!", Courtney stepped through the middle of the mush pot and kissed me.

Courtney Crenshaw *kissed* me.

Courtney kissed *me*!

It wasn't the greatest kiss of all time or anything like that. It wasn't even very long—a blink and everyone else missed it kind of kiss. A quick kiss on the lips, about half the kiss Kayla gave me at the dance.

Kayla. Just thinking her name made me freeze for a second.

Kayla would not be happy about the kiss. But I couldn't think about that right now. No, I needed to shake the noise maker and pretend to sing the song and smile at everyone—not like the dope who just got kissed, but like the cool guy who gets kissed all the time.

The Kiss was nothing like Dante and Gloria's kiss–which ended after I remembered there were other people in the room besides Courtney and me. But it was more than what Juan got, which was Chi's hand pressed firmly to his mouth when he went in for a kiss. No matter how I unpacked the action, the only clear conclusion was that Courtney kissed me.

Once the bad singing and noise making was finished, the group remained standing, so I did too. Courtney talked to her two friends while Gloria, Dante and Juan huddled up, and in hushed voices discussed what to do next. The two eighth grade girls didn't seem to be talking, but they weren't paying any attention to me, who stood there, all alone again.

Alone in this crowd was bad. For one, I was all too familiar with that awkward feeling. But now I also had Courtney's kiss to think about, which regrettably was immediately followed with thoughts of Kayla and the ridiculousness of boyfriends and girlfriends in the seventh grade. It wasn't like we were ever going to get married. Why shouldn't we be able to kiss other people?

I checked my phone for the time: 9:05 pm. Kayla sent a text thirty minutes ago of her, Thea, Aditi and two others dressed in extra-large plastic sunglasses, sparkly top hats, and colorful feather boas. They looked like they were having a blast, whatever it was they were doing.

It was now 9:06 pm.

I had two options. I could sit down and watch everyone talk, and risk it being even more obvious that, despite Courtney's rather friendly kiss, I didn't belong at the party. Or I could go home. Maybe Courtney would walk me to the door like they did in movies and I could ask her what the kiss meant. That's what I would do if she were Kayla.

At 9:08 pm the decision was clear.

"I need to go," I said to the room–and group in general–and waved a short goodbye hand at Courtney.

I half-expected Courtney would point out it was only 9 pm and early for New Years Eve, but she didn't.

She instead said, "Tell Kayla *Hi* and *Happy New Year* for me," and then returned to talk with her friends. She didn't even walk with me to the stairs.

"Later Miller," Dante shouted as I headed for the stairs.

I waved my goodbye to him, then disappeared down the stairs and out into the night. The chilly air enveloped me like an old, familiar friend, the cold air filling my lungs and jumpstarting the rest of me. Instead of walking I jogged through the festive night.

By 9:12 pm I was back in my room and firing up my Xbox.

"I'm back," I said into my headset.

Mitch did his guffaw thing.

Jeff responded with a snarky, "You left?"

TIP #11 AVOID A CLASSIC FAUX PAS

Boyfriend Survival Guide Tip #11 AVOID A CLASSIC Faux pas

For the first day back from winter break, my best but brief answer to the question-of-the-day "How was your break?" was: perfect. We spent four days on Kauai, an "extended weekend" as Mom called it, so my cousin and I stuck to the same spot near the hotel where we could walk out the sliding back door, head down the sandy path, and hit the water within minutes of waking. All four mornings.

Break was sixteen days though, not four, so if anyone wanted to hear about the rest of my break, I told them about the marathon Minecraft game I played with my friends or mentioned in an off-handed kind of way about the father-son outings or about soccer practice, or even about riding my bike to Kayla's to give her the surfing Santa I bought for her.

It never felt like the right time to mention going to Courtney's New Year's Eve party, mainly because it never felt safe, like I could tell one specific person and it not get back to Kayla, because when she asked me what I did on NYE's night, I panicked. While Kayla rang in the New Year at her best friend's sleepover, I really was in the middle of a marathon game of Minecraft with Jeff, Mitch, and more. Totally true. The sixty-six minutes spent at Courtney's New York NYE party didn't affect the actual New Year's celebration for California.

Not mentioning Courtney's party was as easy to do as going to it in the first place—I simply had to do it. I had to go to her party, even though my girlfriend refused to go and thought it would be crazy for anyone to actually *want* to go. I had to go.

I floated through the first half of the day, my Hawaiian tan hardly visible under my hoodie and jeans, but it was there and it was enough to keep me talking about that trip and not about the rest of the break. Not even the cold rain or being forced to eat in The Cave could dampen my mood.

During science though, while we watched a video and took notes on cells, my phone waited impatiently in my lap. We were seven min-utes into the video and still no text from Courtney. Was something wrong? Everything was fine when I left her house after the New York clock struck midnight and after everyone screamed "Happy new year!" and even after she kissed me. Sure, I hadn't heard from her since then, but I was vacationing in Hawaii and biking to Kayla's and watching movies and playing Xbox. She was probably just as busy.

She rarely looked my way before texting, so I wasn't concerned about the lack of visible attention from her. She normally texted first, then later made eye contact or smiled. But without the text at our usual time, I started to panic. Should I have texted her? Some sixth sense said no, even after she kissed me, or maybe especially after she kissed me. Not that the kiss was a big deal. She probably forgot all about it. It was a peck on the mouth, nothing to get all excited and flustered about. It meant nothing to her.

We were well past the ten-minute mark of the video when my cell vibrated. Finally!

> *It was great seeing you over break. Thanks for coming over*

Relief washed over me like a desperately needed wave for surfing. Courtney wasn't mad at me, or done with me; we were all good, and we still had our text thing going on. I quickly typed out my response.

> Me: *It was a great party! Thanks for inviting me.*

The relief from finally hearing from Courtney relaxed me in a way nothing else had that day. I lost myself in frantic note-taking to catch up on the lecture. Many minutes later, the lack of a response from her reignited the worry. Maybe I hadn't said anything to solicit a response. I decided to ask her about her break, but this time I thought long and hard on how to phrase it because I wanted it to be just right.

Once I had my message memorized, I swiped open my phone, just as it vibrated.

> Courtney: *U look tan.*

The *U* in place of *you* was typical Courtney, so why did it look wrong? The line above it was also typical Courtney: *Remember my place NYE. C U there.* It was her reminder text she sent the day before her party.

A sub-zero chill streaked through my body from my head to my toes.

I scrolled up and down, re-reading the most recent texts between us, the chill ruling over all other bodily functions. I closed the chat between me and Courtney. Below her name in the list of most recent text messages was Kayla. But instead of the first part of her emoji filled text from that morning by her name, it showed my last message to her. With the sickest of sick feelings warring with the glacial freeze in my gut, I opened up the chat between me and Kayla.

> Kayla: *It was great seeing you over break. Thank you for coming over*

> Me: *It was a great party! Thanks for inviting me.*

My previously digested lunch broiled in my belly, threatening to resurface. With equal parts fear and dread—there's a distinct difference—I swiveled around to face Kayla. Even in the dark classroom with the only light coming from the video playing on the large screen TV in front, the faint light bounced off Kayla's glassy eyes and confirmed everything.

My mouth opened like I had some idea of what to say, but no words formed because there were no words, there were no ideas, and there were no options.

Kayla, on the contrary, had a much better grip of the situation, better ideas of what to say, and better words to use.

"You asshole."

Two precise, well-thought-out words sliced me to shreds as if she had flung bone-cutting knives at me.

"Miss Burns," called out our teacher from her perch on her desk, "language! Stay after class!"

Kayla rapidly blinked, not looking at me, but at the same time looking at me, and I stared, too stunned for words or action. Her eyes got shinier. Mine got wider, the surge of cold panic still ricocheting through me. Her flushed face grew redder. I lost all feeling in my face.

A single quivering tear escaped over the dam of her lower eyelid, and it was like it was the Pied Piper leading the rats away as a ton of tears followed, streaking down her cheeks.

Then, her hand jerked above her desk, so fast and abrupt, I didn't understand what happened, until the blue Bic pen bounced off my nose.

"Ouch!"

Gasps and some curses dropped like bombs all around me. Ms. Woodson stormed towards us, but before our teacher could reach us, Kayla picked up Jeff's heavy as stone, metal water bottle. *Oh, shit.* I jumped up.

"Kayla! Stop!" our teacher ordered, but her powerless words were as effective as my silent but sincere plea for Kayla to forgive me.

Kayla launched her missile. I barely got my hands up in time to block the bottle from smacking me in the face, but still, the only possible outcome was me landing hard on my butt.

Little squeals and squeaks of shock followed, mixed in with some cheers more appropriate at a WWF match. My table partner further shocked me when he hooked his arm beneath my armpit and hauled me to my feet.

Jeff held Kayla against him, his eyes wider than outer space.

"Stop!" Ms. Woodson stomped to my side. "Mr. Miller, move over there." She pointed to the opposite side of the classroom. "Now!"

Not about to argue, I grabbed my backpack, hugged all my belongings from my desk to my chest, and did as I was told.

Ms. Woodson attempted to quiet the class, but really, how could she stop seventh graders from talking (and texting) about The Attack of the Ticked Off Girlfriend happening in the middle of science class?

Normal teachers would write referrals and send kids to the office. But Ms. Woodson had never been accused of being normal.

Across the classroom, behind my former desk, Jeff helped Kayla stop crying. I had a clear view of how from my new spot. Below the table, he held her hand in his lap, his fingers rubbing her wrist and it looked like so much more than just consoling her. What was my best friend doing?

My phone vibrated against my leg,

Courtney: *Looks like K is mad at U!*

I didn't respond. Kayla was more than pissed, and it went far beyond her idea of Tuck and Alicia "not fighting". It was an epic, name-calling, water bottle-launching, teacher-separated fight. A fight so big, it might be the couples fight-of-the-year, if there was such a thing. The tears streaking down Kayla's cheeks only added additional proof to the reality of the fight.

Courtney: *R U OK?*

I bent over my desk, pretending to look at my notebook, trying to catch my breath. On a scale of 1 to 10, with one being the sludge in a pig pen and ten being awesome, I was in the vicinity of 0.5. I was a long way from OK. I ignored Courtney's second text.

My shoulders still shook with each breath I took, but each breath was a little less labored than the last. My heartbeat raced like it did when I finished suicide sprints at the end of practice. With a couple soccer incidents as the exception, I had never been physically threatened before, certainly not at school, and Kayla's sudden attack had me...a little on edge.

The one thing worse than her attack: my best friend's traitorous actions. After she cussed me out and threw shit at me, Jeff consoled her. I took a long, slightly shaky breath, then pulled up Jeff's contact on my phone.

Me to Jeff: *WTF.*

From the wrong side of class, I watched Jeff and Kayla, silently telling him to look at his phone. But he didn't.

After long moments of waiting for him to respond, I was about to fire off another text his way when Courtney texted me a third time.

Courtney: ☻How can I help?

Courtney Crenshaw offering to help me? And when I needed help, when I needed a friend, more than any other moment in my life? Seeing her offer, understanding it, appreciating it for what it was, I didn't hesitate.

Me: ¯_('~')_/¯

Courtney: *Jamba will cheer you up!*

Me: *Yes!*

TIP #12 BE HONEST

EXBOYFRIEND SURVIVAL GUIDE TIP #12: WHEN IN DOUBT, BE HONEST

For the next day and a half, if the gossip discord app for our school was a search engine, my name would have tallied the most hits. Kayla and my epic breakup was all anyone wanted to talk about Monday after school. Tuesday morning the old school gossip chain picked up where the discord discussion left off the night before.

Being the center of attention and top gossip worthy was a little exhilarating and a lot gut-wrenching, freaking terrifying. It was like being thrust into the school spotlight all alone this time around, against Kayla instead of with her. My social status experienced a wild metamorphosis from nerdy smart kid who voluntarily answered teachers' questions last year to kinda cool kid who constantly answered kids' questions this year.

Was it cool to have wild, epic breakups? At the time it was the worst thing that could happen to me, especially with Kayla hurling water bottles and obscenities at me. But now everyone wanted to know the scoop. Even Dante stopped me during passing period.

"Miller," he shouted, jogging over to me somehow, with his hands stuffed in his jean pockets and his backpack bouncing against his back. "Did Kayla really attack you with your own water bottle?"

"No," I said, quick to correct a mistake. "It was Jeff's."

"Damn," he said, shaking his head in disbelief as he pivoted on his heels to bounce away in the opposite direction, forcing several sixth graders to stop in their tracks to let Dante career by them. "Later, Miller," he shouted over a shoulder.

I wasn't sure what to make of it. I screwed up. Kayla called me on it. Granted she did it in a very public way, so that everyone knew about it, but I didn't understand how that made me cool or someone everyone wanted answers from.

By mid-day Tuesday, as I walked towards the lunch tables, I had accepted my situation, for the most part, and kept my answers short. I didn't elaborate or do anything that possibly looked like bragging. I admitted I probably deserved it when anyone asked. But I stopped short at confessing what I did. I didn't tell anyone about Courtney's party or The Kiss.

I didn't do this for several reasons. One, a confession such as it was felt a whole bunch like cheating, and it felt silly to be guilty of cheating on my *twelve*-year-old girlfriend. Two, in case I was actually guilty of cheating, it would make Kayla the victim, and judging by her attack on me in Science, Kayla didn't do the victim role well. Three, The Kiss clearly meant nothing to Courtney; I was just the only boy available to her in the moment, and nothing between us had changed. So really, I hadn't cheated at all.

As I approached the already crowded lunch tables, my feet slowed like I was walking through quicksand, realizing my automatic trek to

Kayla's table needed a new destination. I stopped at the edge of the outdoor cafeteria, looking for the right group to eat with. For over a year I had always sat with my normal friend group of Jeff and Mitch and a couple others. Now they still sat with Kayla and her friends, and I was public enemy number one there. Plus, I was still pissed with Jeff, who played dumb when he responded to my text, then had the nerve to take Kayla's side in the whole fight. Sitting with her and her friends at lunch only cemented his betrayal.

"Yo, Miller!"

In the center of the lunch area, Dante waved to me from his prime spot. It was happening. Dante Garcia, one of the most daunting, ultra cool eighth graders, wanted me to sit with him.

Without a second thought, I marched over to his table and sat down across from him, and right next to Courtney.

"Hi," Courtney said, smiling at me before turning back to continue talking with Mona and Aurora.

"Did you see the game last night?" Dante asked me.

The game...Dante was a star striker for any soccer team he played for, but that didn't mean soccer was the only sport he played or watched, and I didn't know him well enough to guess which sport he meant, much less which game. If Jeff had asked me this question, because it was January and not baseball season, I'd know he was asking about football.

With playoffs next week, I didn't think a football game was on last night. It could have been a Lakers game, or a Kings game, depending on the sport, or maybe even a college game?

"No, I didn't," I admitted. "What'd I miss?"

Dante laughed. "Not much, but the ten-minute brawl was less than epic what with all their padding and all. You could have used the padding for your fight with Kayla."

I forced a laugh, hoping it sounded casual and not like my heart was in my throat and running a six-minute mile at the moment. Was he making fun of me? Did he only call me over to be a butt of his joke?

But Dante continued, "Hockey's fun, man. It's like soccer but on ice and with sticks."

"And skates and a gnarly ball," Juan said.

"And helmet, shoulder pads, legs pads. Do they have butt pads?" I asked.

The group laughed.

A warm, pleasant flush heated my cheeks.

"They definitely have butt pads," Dante said.

The group laughed again and this time I laughed with them, and all of it, the real laughter bubbling up my throat, the crinkling of skin around the corners of my mouth, and the light almost airy feeling of my chest, all of it wrapped around me in a tight but reassuring hug.

In science Ms. Woodson reminded me of my new seat on the opposite side of the classroom from Kayla. The seat wasn't ideal. I missed my lab partner; he was a little odd and a lot serious, but I liked him. My new lab partner, a girl I knew from the second grade–the one who ate paste and picked her nose–veered between silent as stone to the nosiest person of all time. As hard as it was for me to outgrow the teacher's pet role, I used to sympathize with her challenge of outgrowing the paste-eating, booger-picking role, but as soon as she asked me questions about Kayla, that sympathy evaporated.

Our communication went like this:

"Hi, Sean," she said, twirling long brown hair around her finger while flashing me a full view of her braces with a rainbow of rubber bands, a different color around each brace. "Have you talked with Kayla?"

I stared at her blankly, like the name Kayla confused me.

"Is she still mad at you?"

Darn it, I might have blinked. Don't move a muscle. What was Ms. Woodson doing?

"What did you do to piss her off?"

The effort to maintain the blank stare drained my energy. I couldn't hold out much longer. Why wasn't our teacher talking already.

"Did you—"

I spun around in my chair. I didn't know the boy or girl behind me beyond their names, but at this point I was desperate to escape my partner's grating questions. I asked Carly directly behind me, "Did we have homework last night?"

Carly blinked back at me, her thick black eyelashes weighing down the blink, making it super slow. "*You* are asking *me* if we had homework?"

"Yeah. Did we?"

She shrugged. "I don't know. It's not like I do it."

"Oh."

It wasn't the most encouraging conversation ever, but I was desperate to avoid my new partner so, instead of retreating, I dug in and offered another stimulating question.

"Do you mean, you don't do homework, like at all, or just that you didn't do it last night?" I couldn't look away from Carly and risk paste-eater launching another question at me. I didn't even care if Carly thought I was weird acting like I couldn't live without knowing whether or not she did homework.

Carly stared at me for a couple of rapid-blink seconds, then proceeded to talk to me like I was a simpleton. "I. Don't. Do. Homework. At all. It's only 15% of our grade."

"But...15% is the difference between an A and a B." Stupid, stupid response, but it was out there. Too late to fix. Did everyone believe in the Courtney Crenshaw theory that grades meant nothing in middle school?

Along with the heavy mascara, Carly's eyes were lined in black, which added a touch of drama when she stared at me like she was a jaguar about to pounce. "So?"

Defeated, I turned back around, raising a mental shield to fend off paste-eater's next question, but Ms. Woodson saved me by greeting the class and launching into her lecture. She even managed to show her video on the new Promethean board—which looked like a giant TV screen on a rolling stand—and I took copious notes.

While writing everything Ms. Woodson posted on the Google slide and much of what she said, I peeked over at Kayla and Jeff. Several times they ducked their heads to whisper to one another. Neither were bold enough to laugh during the lecture, but they seemed a little too entertained.

About half way through class, my cell vibrated in my backpack. I totally forgot about Courtney texting me. I pretended to look for an eraser in my backpack in order to pull out my phone again. Courtney's text wasn't much, just a sleep emoji. Trying to match my current state with an appropriate emoji, I responded with the emoji that looked somewhat deranged.

According to Elijah and Antoine, who updated me on my gossip status on the bus ride home, Kayla and my breakup had been bumped out of top spot, replaced with a juicier story: a love triangle starring me, Kayla, and Courtney. It was a role Courtney seemed born to play since she took center stage in the tale with an unfortunate twist ending—The Kiss.

After successfully keeping The Kiss under wraps for almost two full days, it was out there for all to know. And in the story, it doesn't have Courtney kissing me, but just us kissing, leaving it up to the imagination on who kissed whom.

There was no saving my relationship with Kayla at this point, but still, I didn't want anyone to know about the kiss. Maybe because I didn't want Kayla to learn she was right about me all along, that I did still like Courtney and that's why I chose to hang out with her. But I also didn't want the entire school to find out.

Now I was a big fat cheater and the whole school knew it.

Who told? It wasn't Juan or Dante, who were too busy then to notice what I was doing. Plus, that wasn't cool. It was against the bro code. Which meant it was one of Courtney's friends...or Courtney. But why? Could I ask Courtney about it? Was it worth risking upsetting her to get some answers?

I did nothing.

Nothing to defend myself, like tell people Courtney kissed me, not the other way around. Nothing to explain why it wasn't as bad as it looked. Nothing to help Kayla, who no doubt hated being the victim.

My act of inaction made me feel even more guilty.

The upside to all the attention was obvious. I was with Courtney and Dante's crowd. I was with the in-crowd. And wasn't that what I wanted?

I sat with them at lunch. Courtney and I texted in other classes, not just science. I didn't feel an ounce of guilt abandoning Jeff and Mitch who continued to eat with Kayla and her friends anyway.

It wasn't like I had intentionally traded one set of friends for another. More like I had fallen into Courtney's group, except for the fact that her group was a huge upgrade in status.

My first extremely public breakup could have ruined me, but I managed to not only survive, but thrive.

TIP #13 DO BETTER

EXBOYFRIEND SURVIVAL GUIDE TIP #12: ACTIONS SPEAK LOUDER THAN WORDS, SO DO BETTER

Thursday morning marked the end of my time in the gossip spotlight. I was bumped by Dante dumping Gloria sometime after school on Wednesday. Dante's single status spread so fast, by the mid-morning break everyone was talking about it.

I approached the lunch area Thursday hesitantly optimistic. But a quick survey of the area told me my optimism was naïve. Dante and Juan and their friends still sat in the center of the lunch tables, but Courtney with Glo and their friends were many tables removed. This was bad for me for two reasons. One, Dante was the one who invited me to the lunch table, so could I still choose to sit with him? Two, Dante was the one who invited me, so could I still sit with Courtney?

Dante's table was stuffed full of popular and intimidating eighth graders and I didn't see how I would fit in there. Courtney's table at least had space for me and she was a seventh grader. So I opted for what was my best option.

Courtney greeted me as I joined them. She didn't exactly scoot over to make room for me, but there was plenty of room so she didn't need to. I smiled at Aurora, Mona, Glo, and another eighth-grade girl. The girls consoled Gloria the entire lunch. This meant I said next to nothing the entire lunch and just sat there, eating, wishing I had another guy to talk to and wondering what it would be like to sit at Dante's table.

Courtney, Aurora and I walked to science class together. They talked about some celebrity whose name meant nothing to me. Once inside the classroom they kept walking and I sat down next to the paste-eater. She didn't have a hundred questions ready to fire off at me, at least.

Sitting on the opposite side of the classroom from Kayla for the fourth day, I couldn't help but stare for long seconds. Her hair was pulled up in a knot of hair, like Courtney's messy but perfect knots, but I doubted copying Courtney was her intent. Her clothes were also not her norm. Gone were her comfy and bright surf shirts, and instead she wore a dark sweater—it was winter after all—with plaid leggings and black boots. Gold hoops dangled from her ears, circular hoops clinked around her wrist, and a large gold necklace hung from her n eck.

She looked good. She just didn't look like the girl I knew. I missed her easygoing style of dress that perfectly matched her personality. I guess this new look matched the cold, calculated way she treated me now, if ignoring me even counted as treatment.

Just for the heck of it, I fired off another apology text to her.

If she heard her phone alert her to a text, she ignored it.

Friday during lunch, as I approached Courtney's table, I hoped Gloria was doing better, dreading another awkward lunch. As I bent down to sit next to Courtney on the blue plastic bench, she blocked my seat with her leg.

"Oh, Sean, no." She then glanced at each of her friends before looking back up at me. There was no smile. There was no playful pout. There was no warning. "You need to go back to your friends now."

She turned back to her friends, dismissing me as if I no longer stood there frozen in mid hunch about to sit, officially and brutally uninvited. Unaware, unprepared, unsure what to do next. Did she mean for this lunch, or did she mean forever? Her words weren't clear.

But with her back to me, pretending I didn't exist, I couldn't very well ask what she meant. And didn't actions speak louder than words? Surely her actions were clear.

Never before had I wished for the ground to swallow me and hide me from all the all-seeing, prying eyes all around me. Never had I experienced such cold, slap-in-the-face rejection. It stung ten times worse than the hardest kicked soccer ball to the face. Even when Kayla cussed me out and hurled stuff at me, at least she was one hundred percent focused on me. At least I deserved her rage.

Two days ago, Courtney gave me a lifeline; she stepped in as my friend when I most needed one. Now she left me hanging in the worst way, with no place to go. Turning her back on me, when I was still desperate for her friendship, her cold eyes with that cold shoulder of hers. The total rejection was real.

An audience of easily one hundred people watched, everyone eager to welcome me into the spotlight again. I stood as straight as possible. I jammed my hands in my jean pockets. I slunk away from Courtney, her table, and the entire lunch area, with only one wish racing through me. I wished to go back in time to when I was invisible.

Like an avatar killed in a video game, I respawned to the start of the school year with Courtney unaware of my existence. After school I beat a quick path to the bus. Elijah and Antoine saw me in line for our bus and stopped to talk as if I wasn't the school's newest pariah.

More bizarre, Antoine spoke first. "Hey, dude."

"Heard you were Crenshawed," Elijah said, his tone a mix of pity and reverence.

"Is that what happened?"

They weren't the first to talk to me about *The Miller Triangle*. How appropriate: my wrecked social life was being compared to the Bermuda Triangle.

Elijah gave a half shrug, one that was both indifferent and sympathetic at the same time. It was a gesture worthy of imitation.

"It seems to be her thing," he said.

The whole mess was too much for me. I just stared at him, dumbstruck.

"She breaks up couples," he said in a matter-of-fact way.

"What?" I grabbed Elijah's sleeve and tugged him towards me. "Why didn't you say anything? Why didn't you warn me?"

"Hey." Antoine's arm shot forward between us and he jerked his chin at my grasp of Elijah's sleeve.

"Sorry," I grumbled, letting go of his sleeve, but not really feeling my apology.

"We thought you knew. Everyone knows. That's just her M.O."

I shoved my hands in my jeans pockets and stared at my feet. Kayla tried to warn me about Courtney. "Kayla hates me."

"Yep."

A physical pang, like a side cramp while playing soccer, struck below my ribs. I never did anything to Courtney, except worship her from afar—was that a crime worthy of her messed up attack?

"Why me?"

Antoine made a tchaah sound. "Who knows?"

"I think it's more about the girls," Elijah said, but his tone was more like he was hypothesizing an unexpected outcome from a science lab. "Girls that won't play her games." He gave me another mixed shrug. "Girls like Kayla."

Despite his hesitant theory, the sinking sensation in my gut made his words real. If true, it meant Kayla was right all along. About everything. And it meant I was the biggest idiot ever. Even her last words to me rang true. I *was* an asshole.

TIP #14 JUST DO IT: APOLOGIZE

If admitting that I was an asshole was the first step, then I was solidly on to step two. I just didn't know what step two looked like. Was it a planning step or an action step? Was step two about apologizing or was step two more focused on changing one's ways?

I still flat out ignored Jeff at the bus stop. He moved in on my girlfriend literally seconds after we broke up, so *I* wasn't the bad guy in that scenario. More like I did what any betrayed friend would do. In fact, a tinge of pride for standing up for myself fueled my confidence as I bounded up the steps into the bus. Jeff and I normally sat in the middle of the bus, but screw that—I headed three rows past the middle and far closer to the coveted back of the bus.

Elijah sat directly behind me and immediately leaned into the back of my seat. I turned in my seat so that we could nod our hellos. Elijah's smile was an odd one, not unfriendly, but one with some reservations hidden behind it.

"You look like you're in kick-ass mode," he finally said.

"I have a kick-ass mode?"

"Uh, yeah. I see it all the time on the pitch." The pitch was the soccer field, something our British coach insisted we use when we discussed anything related to soccer (but I refused to call the sport football). "Especially during the one v. one drills. Man, I hate going up against you."

"Huh."

This was a new concept to me. I'd always envisioned my life in sections, and each section required a different Sean. I had played soccer since I was five and was one of the more regular captains of my team, which meant I had to set examples and direct players when they needed it. On my team I was kind of a leader. I guess I was a Confident, Take-Charge Sean in soccer. I always upped my game an extra bit during one v one drills–especially the ones that involved both attacking and defending since I was strong at both, but how did that type of intensity–the type I lived for in soccer–relate to this moment seated on the bus going to school?

"Whose ass do I want to kick?"

I could easily picture several opponents my team regularly faced. But in soccer, kicking ass was executing moves to dribble around the guy and hard tackles to stop their attack and recover possession, and sometimes, blatantly fouling, all of which was fun. What did kicking ass look like at school?

I prayed it wasn't literal. While my soccer skills were top-notch, my fighting skills were nonexistent.

Elijah stared at me for another couple seconds before giving me his half shrug.

At the next stop Antoine moved down the aisle with his typical swagger, claiming his normal spot next to Elijah. The second he was seated, Elijah said, "My friend is in his kick-ass mode. Whose ass does he want to kick?"

Antoine did his tchaah noise and without a second thought said, "Courtney."

Jeff was my best friend who betrayed me. He was the one who I just interacted with before sitting down, he was the one I was ignoring. But Courtney... did she deserve more of my wrath than Jeff?

I shrugged, helpless. "I don't know what I would do." Courtney was popular and popularity gave her power–power she obviously abused. Why had I not seen it before? Courtney *was* as manipulative as Elijah, Antione, and Kayla all said she was. How could I possibly compete? I was a big nobody.

"No clue." Antoine voiced my answer and Elijah's slumped but chill posture seemed to agreed. It was unanimous: Courtney was indestructible. But there had to be something I could do.

At lunch that day I sat with Antoine and Elijah and their crew, a louder, larger, and far more noticeable group than my friends and Kayla's friends combined. Like Courtney's table there was a mix of eighth graders with seventh graders, and just like Courtney's table, there were kids like Dante who were good-looking and popular and downright scary. Unlike Courtney's table, laughter and inside jokes and plenty of general joking around was this group's MO.

But I needed advice and I needed it in the next thirteen minutes.

When all the laughter and joking stalled, I leaned closer to Elijah and asked, "Any ideas on how I can get back at *her*?"

"Oh, no you aren't," Shondra said, interrupted us. "Tell me you aren't after payback with that girl."

I didn't know Shondra at all, beyond the basics like she was the second tallest girl at our school and a star volleyball player–do not ask how she dunks–unless you like feeling dirt and want to be educated in the finer aspects of volleyball. If that wasn't enough, she was an eighth grader, so needless to say, she terrified me. The response I needed to give her was obvious.

"Uh... no?"

"Good. Cause that toxic witch will destroy you in seconds."

"But why?" I asked, as if Shondra, this girl who never gave me a second glance before, was the expert on all things Courtney. "Why does she get off on making others miserable? I mean, that's what she does, right? With Kayla, with me, with half this school?"

My legit question managed to keep Shondra's inquisitive brown eyes on me, which probably wasn't my best move of the day. There was an air of authority mixed with indifference when she said, "Well, there's that thing about miserable people wanting company, but maybe she does it just because she can."

"For the power rush," Elijah said, then nodded, as if the more he thought about his words, the more he agreed with them.

It was all so very stupid. Courtney ruined people to make herself feel better? Maybe this was why Kayla disliked her so much. Was it possible *Courtney* was the reason Kayla disliked popularity and trying to *be like the cool kids*. And as if the blindfold had finally been lifted, I realized what Kayla had been hinting at all along: Kayla had been burned before. At the same time, another truth followed: Kayla didn't cower or backdown. Courtney earned Kayla's blatant hostility. Yet more proof I was a jerk.

But I hadn't meant to hurt her. In that one way I was different from Courtney and that made all the difference. I was more than a good soccer player. I was a decent person. Yeah, I screwed up with Kayla, but I didn't set out to hurt her or anyone. I worked hard to be nice to everyone, like Kayla did. I needed to be more like Kayla by the way she stood up to Courtney, too.

The warning bell rang, announcing the end to lunch. I didn't have any idea what to do or say to Courtney, all I knew was that I wanted to do something. I wanted to stand up for myself, and for Kayla, and for anyone else who had been *Crenshawed*. I just didn't know how.

At least I knew what step two was: figuring out what to do next. And I knew to start with Kayla first. When we were given the first ten minutes to write a summary of the lab we did on Friday, I completed mine in two and then spent the next eight minutes writing–yes writing, not texting–an apology letter to Kayla. I risked her chucking it across the room and someone else getting ahold of it and reading it, but I decided I could live with that outcome.

Step three: my awesome (note the sarcasm) first ever apology letter:

Dear Kayla,

You were right about everything, even the rap music played at the Blacklight Blast. But seriously, you were right about Courtney. I can't believe how right you were and I am a total idiot for not listening to you. I didn't want to believe anything bad about anyone, but that was my own stupidity, and you were right about me, too.

OK, as far as apology letters go, mine sucked, but I wasn't sure how to fix it and make it less pathetic, so I continued.

I never meant to hurt you–not at all–and I hope you can forgive me. I hope we can be friends again.

Sincerely,

Sean

Well, while it wasn't Shakespeare or poetic or anything, it was clear and precise and longer than a text. The next obstacle was how to get it to her. The location of the apology, in science class where it all went down, if nothing else, was poetic. And if done right, Courtney would see it.

It was a small, subtle thing, sure, but it felt right, apologizing to Kayla's in an *almost* public way while ignoring Courtney's existence. That was the other part of my apology: showing everyone that Courtney meant nothing to me. My stupid crush on her was so over.

With about a minute left on the timer, it was time to take action. I stood up and walked across the front of the class (something I never willingly did with kids in their seats) under the pretense that I was throwing a piece of paper away, but instead of continuing to the small trash can in the front corner of the class near the teacher's desk, I veered abruptly down the far aisle. As I walked past Kayla's desk, I slipped my folded apology letter beneath her written summary in her notebook. And I kept on walking, all the way to the back of the classroom, then across the back of the classroom, then up the far aisle heading back towards my seat. Then I dropped the tiny speck of trash in the trash can by the door and sat back down.

Fortunately for me, Ms. Woodward didn't start paying attention to me until I reached the back of the class, so she didn't see my true mission, but as it was a bold move and not something I ever do–walking around the classroom without permission–surely those who knew me, or pretended to know me, noticed. I couldn't look at Courtney or her friend and risk ruining my big, daring show of indifference towards her, but I also couldn't risk looking at Kayla either now that the teacher was watching me closely.

I instead ripped my elaborate and painstakingly crafted, two-minute summary out of my notebook. Half a second later the timer finished its countdown on the screen and exploded with victorious music.

My act of defiance wasn't the most heroic and probably wouldn't go down as the most effective way to stand up for oneself, but at least I did something. My main regret was not doing more and sooner. For the first time in months, possibly since I started middle school, I felt a lot more than just a tinge of pride.

I liked the feeling. I wanted to do more.

TIP #15 BE BETTER

The gray clouds blocking out the sun made it seem later than 4 pm as Elijah and I walked home from the nearby park on Saturday, but even with the short days at the end of January, we had plenty of time to get home before dark. We walked and talked and cracked jokes about how bad the other team was. Over the last few weeks since my breakup with Kayla, I spent most of my time, in and out of school, with Elijah and his friends. Kayla never responded to my apology letter, but no one else mentioned it, either, so I had to assume she had it and hopefully read it.

Screeching tires and a loud but familiar rattling thundered from behind us at such a rate we spun around worried we were about to be hit by a car. Tuck's green artifact-on-wheels swerved away from the curb after completing a too wide U-turn before it careened back towards us and the curb.

Elijah swore and jumped back a foot, pulling me back with him.

The tires squealed long and loud as Tuck's car smothered the curb. The car's continuous growl swallowed up the air between us. Tuck crawled out the driver's side window to speak to us over the top of his car, race car style.

"Hey, LD. Haven't seen you in a few days."

A few days was really a few weeks. He looked so different from the Tuck in my memory, it could have been a few years. His hair was longer and shaggier, the curly bangs almost covering his red tinged eyes, and his face was scruffy.

"Hey, get in. I'll give you a ride home."

Reasons to politely reject his offer: one, my house was a five-minute walk away and two, abandoning my friend was not cool. Then again, Elijah's house was even closer than mine.

Reasons to accept his offer: one, Kayla still ignored my existence at school; in science, at lunch, wherever our paths crossed. She continued to look right through me like I wasn't there. Two, not only did I miss Kayla, but I missed Tuck. I even missed Alicia. It would be nice to catch up with Tuck, see how Kayla was really doing, see if she maybe possibly missed me too.

Flashing Elijah my most apologetic smile, I said, "Is it OK if I catch up with you later?"

Elijah's sculpted eyebrows showed his shock.

My smile turned sheepish, but I didn't let his shock deter me. I flung open the door and plopped down in Tuck's car that was all too familiar to me. I hung my hand out the window to wave good-bye to Elijah as the tires squealed. We peeled away from the curb, a strong melted rubber odor filling the inside of the car. As we cruised away from Elijah, who still stood rooted to his spot on the sidewalk, a new, sweet, herbal, almost sticky odor smothered the noxious burned rubber smell. The almost soothing scent encouraged slower, deeper breaths, allowing me to relax to the rhythm of the quivering car. We flew down the road, ten miles over the speed limit, one of Queen's lesser-known songs playing, but since it was a favorite of Tuck's, I was familiar with "Hijack My Heart".

We continued long past the next three intersections, driving in the opposite direction of my house. At the next traffic signal, I spoke up.

"You missed the turn."

"Oh, man. Sorry."

At the next light, we waited in the left turn lane for long minutes that stretched and merged into infinity. While we waited, Tuck's knuckles struck up an agitated beat on his steering wheel, his rapping knuckles in conflict with the song.

After several minutes of waiting for the light to change, he glanced over at me. "Sorry, LD, I've got a lot on my mind."

I nodded. "Yeah, no. I get it."

Finally, the green left arrow appeared, and I braced myself for the car to whip around in a quick U-turn, but instead it turned left. As if the Gremlin had a mind of its own, it drove us past the turnoff to my school. I wasn't all that familiar with the neighborhood past my school. The main thing I didn't know was if there was a way to reach my house on the current street. Tuck drove up the street that might mark the border of Central Valley, with houses on one side and nothing but an immense, barren greenish hill on the other.

"Have you driven here before?"

"Sure," Tuck answered almost before I finished asked my question.

To describe Tuck as suspicious would be a severe understatement. He was very off and I didn't know what to do to snap him out of it.

"OK," was all I said.

His car continued to climb up the street. We passed another street to the left that led into the neighborhood, but it didn't promise to lead us through to the main street that would take me home.

My relaxed state from earlier had evaporated, leaving an uncomfortable tightness in my gut that felt a lot like when I had to present a project in front of the class.

"So…" I started, pushing my back into the backrest, trying my best to fake a relaxed state. "You have a lot on your mind…?"

Tuck's drumming hand paused and hovered an inch above the wheel, fingers splayed straight as if he couldn't both drum and think at the same time. "Yeah."

That's all he said. But his hand finally gripped the wheel again.

A few soccer field lengths ahead of us, the street disappeared as it crested the top of the hill. While I knew the road continued, I couldn't shake the feeling that we were barreling toward the edge of a cliff like Wylie Coyote chasing the Road Runner. All the abuse Wylie Coyote went through because of the clever Road Runner never set right with me, and I really didn't enjoy relating to the classic cartoon villain at the moment.

Why did I get in his car? It wasn't like I needed the ride; I was almost home. I didn't need all this…but then I remembered exactly why I accepted a ride home with Tuck.

"How's Kayla doing?" I even added a blink-rate fast, "I miss her." There, I said it. The main reason I got in his car. "I really want to be friends again. Can you please tell her?"

"Sure." Tuck kept nailing the one-word, terse responses. But they were so un-Tuck like.

A long silence followed his last word. He continued to stare at the empty street ahead of us, but since it was like we were driving off the map in the Timbuktu of Central Valley, there was nothing really to watch.

And we crested the hill. And just what I dreaded to see.

A dead end.

Two lanes on each side of the road and it just ended. Fortunately the center median filled with azaleas ended at the top of the hill, allowing Tuck to execute his squealing tires U-turn.

But instead of cruising back down the hill, he swerved to the side of the road—as if someone would need to pass us.

"I hate it here."

I certainly wasn't a fan. "We just need to go back down the hill to the light. Well, the second light, the one after we pass my school."

"Alicia's pregnant."

Uh... "Oh."

Tuck's hand, the one that had drummed on the wheel, started alternating between flexing and curling up in a fist.

Tuck said he'd talk to Kayla for me. I got what I wanted. What I had initially wanted, back before I got in his car. Now? I wanted to be anywhere but here. Years later, when I looked back on the moment, I would have a million better responses. But at the moment, I didn't have a clue.

But then I had that lightning bolt realization, the one that suddenly seemed so obvious I didn't know how I didn't see it sooner.

Tuck needed a friend.

He sought me out as his friend.

I needed to do better.

"What are you going to do?" My shaky, squeaky voice wasn't ideal.

"What should I do?"

"Um... uh...I don't know..."

I needed to do better.

"Maybe marry her?"

Tuck turned on me then, his eyes flashing anger, but they were shiny, too.

"I can't do *that*. She's way too good for me. She doesn't deserve being stuck with me."

Tuck looked like he was drifting away on an angry cloud of anguish.

"Oh...so then did you break up?" Unlike the rest of his problems, I had experience in breakups.

"Not yet. But it's only a matter of time. We fight a lot."

His ominous, hopeless tone sucked out what little joy had been fighting for survival in his eyes.

I needed to be better.

"Have you told Alicia how you feel? I don't think she'd agree."

His shoulders slumped as if in tune with his long, hopeless sigh.

"She doesn't. Which is one of the many things we fight over."

Yeah. I was not exactly a contender for talking someone down from the ledge.

Digging deep into my stored memories, I searched for Tuck's hopes and dreams or even things he showed an interest in besides Queen. I replayed the last few conversations I had with Tuck, like the one on the way to my house the last time.

The time before that, though, Tuck and I talked about his work, which he hated, and his plans for after high school, or rather, his lack of plans. He had no desire to go to college, even the local community college, nor did he plan on working at Taco Haven. The only things I knew he liked didn't seem all that important right then. He liked reading. He liked listening to music. He liked driving his car. And he loved his girlfriend.

My big discovery of the moment was not the answer Tuck was hoping for, nor was it about Tuck at all. I needed to do better, but where I really needed to do better was in the friend department. Tuck had helped me out a lot while I was with Kayla, driving me home, giving me advice, making me laugh, and just being there when I had dinner with Kayla's parents.

I hadn't realized how much I appreciated him until that moment. I also hadn't realized before then how little I knew about Tuck beyond being Alicia's boyfriend. I needed to be a better friend.

That's when my brain finally stumbled across a fact that could help.

"Hey, why don't we go to the beach sometime?"

Tuck's eyebrows raised in disbelief as he angled his body towards me. "The beach? Really?"

"Yes, really. You don't need to know how to swim to enjoy the beach. You haven't lived until you've run away from the waves crashing on the shore."

He cocked his head to one side, as if thinking it over. "You think?"

"I know." I grinned at him. "And if you won't want to drive, I'm sure my mom or dad will drive us."

The screwed-up face he made was hilarious. I laughed as he said, "Thanks, but no thanks. I can drive." Several seconds passed as he stared back at the empty road ahead of us. Then he said, "Maybe KB will join us."

President of the United States was more likely to join us, but I said, "Yeah, that'd be great," because it would be great if Kayla joined us. But the realist in me added, "Or my friend Elijah could join us. He's not a surfer, either."

After another minute, with the car still in park by the side of the curb, I gently said, "Now can you take me home?"

"Oh," he said, giving his head a good shake as if to clear his thoughts. "Sure, sure. Sorry about all this."

"It's OK—as long as you get me home soon. I hope I helped."

"Yeah." He cranked the key in the ignition and the Gremlin roared back to life. "You helped." He shoved the gearshift into first gear and soon enough, the car crept forward.

As we rolled down the hill towards my school, Tuck fumbled with his iPod until another classic hard rock band, Mötley Crüe, played "Home Sweet Home."

TIP #16 LEARN FROM MISTAKES

One warmish day after school, Elijah and I were shooting baskets in my driveway, just talking and shooting. No dribbling or a passing or anything that felt like exercise. The little white and pink flowers nearby were in full bloom, stinking like a giant bouquet of lilies that taunted my nose.

"So," Elijah said, before bouncing the ball by his feet a few times. He grabbed the ball and assumed the shooting position with a leg tucked in, both bent a bit at the knee. "When are we going to the beach?" He shot the ball with one hand guiding the ball, the other one providing the power.

I hadn't heard from Tuck since that day in his car over a month ago. This surprised me because I thought we had a solid plan to go to the beach. Elijah even agreed to go with me. I couldn't shake the freaked out feeling I experienced when Tuck continued to drive away from, not towards, my house, so I really didn't want to go with just Tuck. Having a friend with me would help me feel safer—safety in numbers, the more the merrier, something like that.

Elijah scooped up his rebound and tossed it to me.

I caught the ball and grasped it with my fingertips. Everyone played basketball during recess in the fifth grade, so I knew the basics, but I didn't take to it like I took to soccer or even baseball.

"I haven't heard from him."

It wasn't until a couple of days later that I realized I didn't have Tuck's number and had no way of contacting him. I suspected he was in the same position, but he could always ask Kayla for my number. Or even Mom, but I'm not sure how comfortable she was giving my personal information to her students, so that might not have worked.

My fingertips pressed into the nubby texture of the basketball for a few seconds before I passed the ball, with both hands, at the basket. One of my favorite things to do in soccer was shoot. It didn't matter how many times or in how many ways—right foot, left foot, head, sliding shot, volley, half volley—scoring a goal was the best feeling in the world. Shooting and scoring baskets, in comparison, was a nonevent. Of course, I didn't make half the baskets Elijah did.

The ball careened off the rim and shot back at me. I caught it and tossed it to Elijah.

Elijah repeated his process. He bounced the ball and with each bounce, an echo bounce followed, so it sounded like six bounces instead of three. He found his preferred grip with one hand guiding, the other hand lifting. Then he said, "Cool. But I'm kinda wanting to go, you know?"

Then he shot another basket.

He retrieved the ball and fired it at me. I caught it with my fingers in perfect formation to cushion it in my fingertips. Shooting baskets might not do it for me, but I liked passing the ball. It was a different skill set from passing in soccer, using hands instead of feet, and yet it was almost calming.

"Yeah, I know. It'd be cool to go without my parents or your parents."

"You should call him."

I bounced the ball once. "I already told you, I don't have his number."

"Your mom's his teacher. Can't she get it?"

I shook my head before lobbing the ball at the basket. It went in with a quiet swish of the net.

"Nothing but net—nice!"

"My mom avoids stuff like that with students."

I tossed the ball back to Elijah and watched him do his routine. Every time. Three bounces, assuming the shooting position, saying something to me, and then shooting.

But before he could say whatever it was he was going to say, a low growl rolled up the street behind us. Recognizing the sound, I spun around.

There it was, Tuck's Gremlin, heading towards us as if we summoned it.

Elijah stood next to me with the ball silenced in the crook of his arm.

We watched the car roll to a stop by the curb in front of us.

Tuck reached over to roll the passenger window down. "Hey, LD."

Three things struck me at once: the alert look about him, the scent and the silence. Tuck's gaze was almost piercing, the whites of his eyes were white, not pink. A strong lemony scent spilled out of the car and surrounded me as if to form a protective shield from the obnoxious flowers. Finally, the only noise inside the car was the old engine chugging. I couldn't remember a time when Queen or another classic hard rock band wasn't playing in his car.

Except for the dark smudgy skin beneath his eyes, he looked good–so much better than the last time I saw him.

Tuck jerked his chin like kids at school did in passing. "Can I give you a ride home?"

Iron fingers tickled my gut. Just the suggestion of that last ride made me feel trapped.

Before I could speak, he laughed and said, "Just kidding, LD."

"Uh, funny."

His brown eyes met mine, and with Tuck, when he looked at you, he really looked at you with soul-searching eyes. Me, I must have been extra observant that day, because I noticed more beyond the odd lack of Queen music blasting from his iPod. Despite it being in the middle of the week, school papers and books didn't litter the tiny backseat.

Despite his bad joke, he wasn't smiling.

"Yeah, so... I'm sorry about last time. I don't know what I was thinking, messed up and all."

I nodded again, but this time I found the words and force them out. "It's OK. You weren't... you."

He looked away, stared at his silent, ancient radio, but when he looked back, his stare was even more intense. "Did you really mean it, about going to the beach?"

"Of course." A long silence filled the space between us. "Elijah wants to come."

On cue, Elijah perked up next to me. "Yeah, the last time I went was like six years ago."

Tuck glanced at Elijah and stared for a few moments.

"Oh, uh, sorry, this is Elijah," I said in an awkward introduction, waving a hand at my friend. I repeated the process in reverse. "Elijah, this is Tuck."

They each said, "Hey."

I didn't know what to say after that. As the silence stretched, it was as if I was back in his car parked on that empty road, grasping for something to say. "So...the San Clemente pier is one of my favorite spots, or we could go to Laguna Beach–they're both about thirty minutes from here. We could get a Scrappy Dog and eat on the beach."

Both Elijah and Tuck nodded, agreeing with my plan.

"Well, let's go then," Tuck said.

"Right now?" He couldn't be serious. But he nodded as if that should have been obvious.

"Oh, uh... my parents won't let me. Not with school tomorrow..." And I doubted we could find a hot dog stand on a weeknight in early March.

"Oh, *parents*. I forget about that."

Tuck's comment triggered an idea I'd been wrestling with lately. I knew his dad had left a long time ago, but suddenly I had to ask, "Where is your mom?"

He answered without hesitation in an almost automated response sort of way. "She works."

"Yeah, you keep saying that. Where? Kentucky?"

His eyebrows shot up, but then the corners of his mouth tilted up. "Kentucky? Of all places, you pick Kentucky?"

I shrugged. Maybe it was the most random state I could think of, but I said, "So not Kentucky?"

"Maybe," Tuck finally said. His eyes had shifted away from me and were instead staring at the space where a radio would have gone, if his car had one. "Yeah, Kentucky's as likely as anywhere else."

"You mean you don't know where your mom is?"

He shrugged, a much heavier action than my shrug. "I haven't heard from her in a while. She calls every so often, from here or there, hasn't stated where in over a year, but her location used to change so much, that by the time she told us where she was, it was where she'd been two weeks ago, or something like that." He shrugged again, as if not knowing where his mother lived was the equivalent of not knowing if he wanted to eat at Burger King or McDonalds.

"Ah, no worries, LD, OK? I'm fine. My younger brother and I live with my older sister and her boyfriend. It's all good."

When he said nothing else, just continued to tap the steering wheel while gazing at me. I said, "OK."

Elijah bounced the ball once, a softer echo than before following.

Tuck gave his head a sudden shake as if the bouncing ball woke him up.

"You're a good kid, LD," he said. "I don't want you making any of the mistakes I did. Don't be in a hurry to grow up, you know?" He reached into a plastic bag, then pulled out an object with a cord–his iPod. "I want you to have this," he said, flashing his silver iPod at me, then dropping it back in the bag. "It's old, doesn't hold its charge, so you have to charge it pretty much all the time, but I've got tons of good playlists, full of uplifting songs. Some bands besides Queen, even." He flashed me a brief smile, then leaned across the passenger seat to hand me the bag.

Dad couldn't bring himself to part with his old iPod, so he gave it to me. It was tucked away in my sock drawer. Not knowing what else to do, I took Tuck's, but the last thing I needed was a second iPod to store in my crammed sock drawer. Especially when Tuck used his all the time.

"But how will you listen to your music?"

Tuck tapped his head with a finger and winked at me. "Got it all stored here. It's all good. I reset the code to 987654."

I stared down at the contents of the plastic bag: a white charging cable wrapped meticulously around the iPod.

"Later, Little Dude. Be good."

"Bye, Tuck."

His forest green Gremlin growled as it pulled away from the curb and roared back down the street. An overwhelming sense of dread spread from some deep crevice inside me. Something profound just happened. I just didn't understand exactly what it was.

Tuck and his Gremlin reached the end of the street, the left blinker signaling, then the car turned the corner. I could barely see Tuck through the driver's side window and then the Gremlin and Tuck disappeared.

Elijah joined me at the curb. "What was that all about?"

I held up the plastic bag. "I think it was an apology?"

The questioning look Elijah gave me mirrored my thoughts. But before I could process everything, he said, "I didn't hear a day planned for the beach."

"Ah, man. I forgot. Next time."

TIP #17 BE A FRIEND

My breakup with Kayla was old news in every way and every place except science, which was by far the worst class ever. Jeff, Kayla and I no longer joked our way through class. Ever since she hurled water bottles and curses at me, Ms. Woodson kept us separated on opposite sides of the room. This did not keep people from gleefully rehashing Kayla's "savage" attack on me, which had decreased to a couple times a week instead of daily, but it still seemed like it was on an invisible group checkoff list.

All this meant every time someone caught me looking over at Kayla, I risked some moron shooting off his mouth. And when they said something humiliating and stupid, Kayla ignored them and their laughter just like she ignored me. I ceased to exist to her the day we broke up. At first it was embarrassing, me saying *Hi* and her acting like I was invisible. Then I tried making it a game and failed miserably at it. Eventually I accepted defeat and stopped trying. I was dead to her.

Over the last few months, I had grown rather adept at avoiding Kayla's side of the room, but from the moment she walked into science class that Wednesday my eyes kept rebounding back to her like a pinball.

Maybe it was the black sweater with super long sleeves. Maybe it was the skintight black pants. Maybe it was her brand new Vans. Or maybe it was the entire ensemble that looked so un-Kayla like, but whatever it was, I couldn't look away for more than a minute. Maybe it was the rapid tapping of her checkerboard-print Vans. Maybe it was her unusually dark lashes with what looked like smudges on her lower lids. And maybe it was the foreign frown tugging her mouth down. No matter how pissed she was at me, except for that horrendous blow up in class that one day, she'd always looked fine, in control and at ease, in class. This current Kayla couldn't be more different from the easygoing surfer girl I dated just a few months ago.

This new Kayla drew my attention like the world's most powerful magnetic. I couldn't look away. I really couldn't think of much else for more than a second or two.

It was the longest science class ever.

Worse, every single time I caught myself staring at her, I caught Jeff staring back at me.

Jeff was another headache entirely. Every time I caught him glancing at me, I'd flip him off. I bet he wished I'd ignore him. He and Kayla lasted maybe a week before she moved on. Was one week really worth throwing away our five-year friendship?

But move on she had and she scored big time. Juan Mendoza, Dante's best friend and the second most popular boy in school, had marked her as his at the Winter Dance. I didn't even go to the dance, but I had heard all about it from Elijah and Antoine. They, along with the rest of the school, were shocked by Juan's interest.

But I remembered how he watched her that day in Courtney's pool and how he asked me about her. He made his interest in her clear that day. While his interest in Kayla didn't surprise me, her interest in him was shocking. Juan was everything she hated about popularity. He made fun of and picked on any unfortunate nerd or loner who crossed his path. But maybe her appearance wasn't the only thing changing?

While debating between flipping him off, which he totally deserved, and the likelihood of getting caught, which I really didn't deserve, I watched Kayla for far longer than recommended. She and Jeff had talked at the beginning of class, but I didn't think she'd said anything to him in a long time, which was as unusual as her outfit and makeup.

This new Kayla was a puzzle I couldn't solve, and the sense of helplessness gnawed at me. It reminded me of how helpless I felt in Tuck's car, not knowing what to say to make him feel better. Why did all these random occurrences make me feel like a terrible friend?

But I did feel like a terrible friend. Having Elijah and Antoine step in as my closest friends at school was nothing less than the best thing to ever happen to me. I needed friends, real friends, and they were there for me. Their friendship reminded me of what being a real friend was about and reminded me of all my shortcomings in the friendship department lately.

The clock above the white board ticked ever so slowly around. Twenty-two minutes to go, then I would be free from science for twenty-three hours.

I physically escaped science, but that antsy, nervous sensation clung to me for the rest of the day with sharp talons. Just before dinner, Mom's tense tone calling me to come downstairs was just another warning bell to sound in my head.

I found Dad seated at the counter on a barstool, Mom standing opposite him in the kitchen, frowning at each other, my mom with glassy looking eyes like she had been crying.

"What's wrong?" I asked, but I didn't want an answer–not if it would make me feel as miserable as they looked.

"Son, we need to talk," Dad said, standing with a firm hand landing on my shoulder to guide me to the barstool next to him.

I slid onto the barstool. Dad remained standing next to me. Mom walked towards the sink, looking from me to Dad. Mom, normally a steel vault with masking her emotions, looked pale and tense.

The kitchen, the whole downstairs, crackled with tension. What was going on? I'd seen and heard my parents fighting before, but it was just normal stuff. But this...this was something very different. Mom and Dad's tense faces combined with the awful tension in the room spelled bad news. I heard enough stories, and saw enough movies...Was my entire world about to change?

Mom's mouth dropped to speak and every muscle in my body tensed.

"Tuck's missing."

My brain glitched. Her words made no sense. How was all this about Tuck?

"Have you seen him or heard from him?"

"Tuck?" It wasn't like Tuck and I texted or chatted online or anything. But Mom's face was pale, the fine lines by her eyes deeper than normal, making her look so serious and worried.

"You mentioned seeing him recently...going to the beach...?"

This was really about Tuck. All the tension, all the alarm, all the worry was for Tuck. I took a slow, steadying breath. I stretched my neck, little bones or tendons cracking, help my body ease into a more relaxed state. Last time I saw Tuck was fifty yards from my kitchen, in front of my driveway. He looked far better than that day a few weeks ago. He apologized. He gave me his iPod, which was an odd thing to do, but I figured he felt really bad about the other day. And we made plans to see each other soon.

"We *talked* about going to the beach. He, Elijah and me. We haven't *gone* yet."

Mom glanced at Dad. Her lips pressed together so tightly they created a deep shadow in the crease. "Did it seem like he might...run away?" Although her complexion was pale and her mouth pinched in, Mom's glassy eyes peered into my soul for answers.

"Run away? No." Tuck was more adult than child, so the idea of him running away sounded ridiculous.

Dad's arm wound around my shoulders and gave me a tight squeeze.

Just to be crystal clear, I asked, "This is all about Tuck? Not about you..." I couldn't finish my thought out loud, both embarrassed by being wrong but also not wanting to give them any ideas. *Please, please don't get divorced!*

"We're worried. That's all." Dad now squeezed Mom's shoulder.

"Maybe he went somewhere? Maybe he drove to the beach without me?"

But Mom shook her head. "No one's seen him in two days. Not his family, nor the Burns. He hasn't been at school. It's just so unlike him. It's like he's just disappeared."

"Well, I'm sure he'll turn up," I said.

Mom walked around to my side of the counter and hugged me, and Dad hadn't stopped his one arm hug, so it became a group hug, my parents clinging to me as if I might disappear, too.

Later in my room upstairs, I couldn't stop thinking about Tuck's odd disappearance. Two days. Where could he be? Was this what was bothering Kayla? She always acted so annoyed by Tuck, like Tuck was an annoying older brother, but she was surely worried about him.

As soon as Kayla entered my brain, I couldn't think of anything else. She hadn't responded to any of my texts since our breakup. She ignored my phone calls. My best apology, the letter, might have earned me the tiniest of smiles, maybe a brief acknowledgement, but I also might have imagined it.

But I had to speak to her. Or at least attempt to speak to her. Let her know I was worried about Tuck, too.

Determination powered my movements. I pulled up her contact in my phone, ready to push the dial icon, but then hesitation won out. For two months, Kayla had acted like I was invisible. She looked right through me when I spoke to her and ignored all my texts. Would she really respond now?

But I had to try. That's what a friend would do, and that's what I wanted to be: a good friend. I pressed the call button. As the phone rang, I ran through my rehearsed speech.

My call went straight to voicemail.

I hung up and texted her instead.

> Me: I just heard Tuck's missing. I'm worried, too. Please call me.

Surprise, surprise: when I went to bed that night, I still hadn't heard from her.

TIP #18: BE BOLD

The next day, I did something I hadn't done since the day Kayla broke up with me. With squared shoulders and a super fake confidence I could only wish I had, I walked over to her group that morning before school.

I could do this because she was back with her *besties,* Thea and Aditi, who were stationed on either side of Kayla, more like buffers than bodyguards as they were both shorter and frailer than Kayla. It was good seeing the three back together again after a couple of bizarre weeks of Kayla and Brit hanging with Dante and Juan's crowd, a crowd I never would have walked up to—not after Courtney brutally dismissed me without a second thought. Jeff and Mitch also returned to hanging with Kayla's group after a brief, mysterious separation—was it because of Juan?

None of that stuff mattered. I needed to talk to Kayla. And this was the best chance and best place and surprisingly least public way to do it.

Her group stood in their usual huddle near the outskirts of the courtyard by the math classrooms in building A. Thea's hands flew back and forth in the air like she was casting an intricate spell while the rest watched her intently.

It was about to get really, really awkward.

I stopped and stood inches behind Jeff and Thea as she continued to talk and gesture, clearly telling a captivating story. Ugh, was everyone so enthralled with her story they wouldn't even notice me? Extra awkward.

Aditi and Kayla turned to gawk at me, Kayla's mouth gaping open, her eyes widening, and like the wave at a ballgame, everyone else followed Kayla's gaze and turned to stare at me as Thea's story stopped mid word.

Yep, a little bit beyond the most awkward moment of my life.

"Hi," I said with a weak wave and a pathetic smile.

Silence welcomed me back to the group.

Screw it. I met Kayla's alarmed gaze with my own hopefully determined one and grasped the straps of my backpack like it was a security blanket. "Can I *please* talk to you?"

She stared back with a million different reactions: shock, anger, and confusion competing to dominate her facial expression while her body shifted between solider-straight and slumped confusion. Yet another refusal was in the making.

A sour desperation rose in my throat. "It's about Tuck." My eyes pleaded with hers. *Please talk to me.*

Again, her shoulders slumped forward. I held my breath, praying the defeated body language was a *good* sign.

"Fine," she said. The look in her blue eyes was more challenge than defeat.

But it was the best I could hope for. I angled my body away from the group and waited.

"Wait for me?" She asked her friends. "This will be quick."

"Of course," Aditi said immediately.

But Kayla stepped away from the group and joined me to walk further away, and that was the best result I could hope for.

We stopped twenty feet away from the group, right next to the Algebra classroom, where I leaned against the side of the building for support.

"My mom told me Tuck's missing?"

She bit her lip and nodded while her eyes searched mine for answers to questions I didn't know.

"I don't understand..." I started, but lost my train of thought as I stared too deeply into her eyes filled with hurt and betrayal. I gulped and tried again. "What happened to him?"

Her head cocked to one side with a suspicious scowl. "I don't know. No one knows, that's the problem."

I shrugged and lifted my hands in a helpless, pathetic plea. "I don't understand why...or how...or anything, really. Should I be...really worried?"

She let out a heart-heavy sigh. "I don't know. Alicia's a mess. They've been fighting, and he hasn't been to our house in a while, but he hasn't been to work, or school, or his own house... No one has seen him."

I shook my head, miffed. "I am so sorry." I wish there was more to say, or a better way to convey how sorry I really was. "I'm sure he'll show up. Hopefully, today."

Kayla blinked rapidly, her eyes a little glassy, but then she nodded.

We stood there for a couple more beats, her staring at the ground by my feet, working hard to not cry, while I stood leaned against the wall, willing her to look at me again. I knew the precious, hard-earned time with her could end at any second and there was one more thing I had to say out loud to her, face to face.

"You know I'm really, really sorry about—well, about everything I did wrong...with Courtney and with you. I really screwed up and I really regret it."

Her mouth curved into a frown that was foreign on her face just a few months ago. "OK."

I sighed, sending warm air up past my nose and ruffling my bangs a bit. The weakest smile ever responded to her accepting my apology. Sensing my time was up and having achieved all I hoped to do with our talk, I tried to end in a way that would set us up for another talk soon.

"Let me know if you hear anything about Tuck, OK?"

"OK," she said again, then nodded a quick goodbye before hurrying back to her friends.

It wouldn't go down as the greatest talk ever, but the important thing was we talked. Finally. And I couldn't ignore the swell of pride inside. I made that happen. I was both brave and considerate of her feelings. And she finally accepted my apology.

That night during the middle of dinner with my parents, I received a text. It was a text I had been hoping to hear for weeks with Kayla's specific ring tone.

Mom had a hard, fast rule about no phones at the dinner table, unless we were eating out at a restaurant, but I knew Mom would make an exception if it was about Tuck.

> *Kayla: Tuck's back, the bastard.*

> *Me: Great news!*

> *Kayla: I'm so mad at him for making everyone worry. But he's here at the house.*

"Tuck's at the Burns' house," I reported to my parents.

Mom's entire body relaxed as if she was an inflatable Christmas decoration just unplugged for the night. I assumed I could continue texting Kayla.

> *Me: Where was he?*

> *Kayla: Says he was visiting family in Tehachapi. No cell reception. ¯_('~')_/¯*

> *Me: I'm so glad he's OK*

> *Kayla: We'll see about that. My Dad's pissed.*

As I relayed the information to my parents, my cell continued to ding.

> *Kayla: My mom's pissed. Alicia's super pissed.*

> *Kayla: Tuck may be back, but he's far from OK.*

But he was back, and back at the Burns' house, so that sounded pretty good to me. My parents agreed. Even better, his disappearance was the key to unlock Kayla's heart and allow her to actually talk with me and accept my apology. Maybe even forgive me?

TIP #19 BE RESILIENT

After the Tuck scare, everything else that was wrong in my life was insignificant. So what if the girl of my dreams used me and discarded me like trash? At least I had new, better friends that I actually felt comfortable around. And while it required a serious scare to get Kayla to talk to me, at least we finally talked and moved past our problems.

My life eased into a calm pattern like elevator music, calm but predictable, drama-free but also kind of empty. Life as Kayla boyfriend had been complicated but exciting, and Courtney and her group added a lot of drama but also opportunity. Now every day was like the last and the next.

However, Monday at lunch, when I sat down next to Elijah, over the top of my lunch bag, I found a new face staring at me.

"Oh, hi," I cleverly said. Well, at least my smile worked.

The mystery girl across the table gave me a small, shy smile.

"Oh, yeah," Shondra said, abandoning her conversation with the girls to her right to point at me with a super long, super bright orange finger nail, "Zoey, this is Sean, the soccer fanatic I told you about." Then Shondra's intense eyes met mine. "This is Zoey."

That's all the introduction I got.

Where Shondra was six feet of attitude, intimidation, and athletic dominance, Zoey looked petite and meek next to her, which wasn't very fair to her since everyone looked meek next to Shondra. But Zoey's eyebrows, so perfect they looked painted on, raised with a hint of interest at the word *soccer* and her amber eyes widened with clear amusement at *fanatic*.

Elijah half jabbed me with his elbow and said, "She's new."

Zoey smiled, her face brightening at a better explanation of her presence. "I have a couple of classes with Shondra. I'm from LA."

I blinked. "LA? Like for real LA or like Hawthorne or Glendale?"

She gave me a withering look that made me feel puny. "LA proper B." Oh, nothing meek about her. For Shondra to approve, she had to have an attitude.

"It's just, well, I never met someone from LA before."

Zoey's perfect eyebrows arched high as she looked from Shondra on her right to another eighth grader on her left. "He's trippin' right?"

Shondra, to her credit, backed my thoughtless comment. "Girl, we don't go there, and they don't come here."

"It's an hour away," Zoey said with a mixture of disbelief and disgust.

"At midnight," was my reflex response.

The entire group laughed except Zoey, but she was new, so she didn't know that's what we did at lunch. Laugh.

Across from me Zoey bit her lip, her downcast eyes staring at her half-eaten turkey and cheese sandwich.

Shondra leaned over the table and told us, "Zoey still plays for her club team in LA. That's why my girl is five kinds of panic right now."

It was my turn to wear the sky-high eyebrows. "You play club soccer?"

The new girl shrugged, but then a hesitant smile appeared and I noticed her pretty pinkish-orange shade of lipstick matched the letters on her hoodie. "I've been with my team for five years now."

"Me, too. I mean, I've been on my team for five years. What position do you play?"

"Striker mostly, but sometimes I'll play winger or midfield."

"I play center mid." My big, dopey grin was out of control, but I didn't dim it a bit. "Elijah plays most every position; he's even our backup keeper." But before her attention shifted to Elijah, I continued, "What level do you play? Our team is gold right now, but we might move up to Premier this summer."

Zoey nodded again, a cute little tilt up and down of her chin, her eyes once again open with interest. "We're in gold right now, but just barely, and if I leave... well, my team needs me."

"Yeah, I get it." I thought about the long practices I went to three days a week and tried to picture driving an hour (at best) to practice and then another hour home, three nights a week. Some separate conversation was happening around us, but I was far more interested in the new girl who, with all her makeup and extensions and all, looked more like a cover model than a middle school student.

This time around, I recognized the swell in my chest and the light-headedness. Hope soared inside, and while the rational side of me must have realized liking an eighth grader was asking for trouble, the fact was Zoey was The New Girl at school, an unknown, a mystery, gave me hope. Most importantly, she didn't have a trail of battered hearts and dreams behind her.

Dating in middle school was awkward, but if I were honest with myself, I had to admit I missed having someone I was supposed to text and talk to regularly. I even missed the holding hands and being a couple, like we were more powerful united as one. At least, that's how it felt when I was with Kayla. And I definitely missed Kayla. I was determined to do better the next time, to be a better boyfriend, and to be a better friend.

Before I lost her attention or my nerve, I asked, "Will you ever have a game near here so I can watch you play?"

Zoey's styled eyebrows straight from a famous work of art shot up for a millisecond before settling back down. Her eyes might have narrowed slightly, but I still could see the golden flecks mingling with the light brown amber. She gave me a slow, teasing smile. That's another thing I liked about her. She had a hundred different smiles, and I liked every single one of them.

"I'm sure I will. You want to come cheer for me?" Her teasing smile reached her eyes.

"Of course." I didn't let the details get in my way of showing my interest.

"I hear you're very dedicated and train on your own a lot during the summer. Maybe we can train together?"

"Oh, yeah. That would be great." This time, I couldn't ignore the details. "I mean, I surf a lot in the summer, so it's afternoons and juggling or shooting, nothing too intense."

Elijah turned in his seat to include us in his conversation with the rest, except then he said, "And Sean has a pool, so afternoon workouts in the summer are lit."

"Boy, do I have to learn soccer now?" Shondra asked, giving me her stare that could freeze the sun. But then she laughed. "I primed this body for bump-set-spike and occasional dives onto hardwood floor. I am not about to hit a ball with my *head.* "

"Uh, no, you don't need to play soccer to, um, come over for a swim." I looked at Elijah, not sure what he was all about–he'd only been in my pool at soccer parties. Our friendship was new, so it wasn't like he practiced with me and went swimming with me last summer, although it sure sounded like a great plan for this summer. Maybe this was his way of making me officially in his group? "I'll have you all over sometime next month."

Shondra gave me her nod of approval.

On one hand, I could see how this group had similarities to Dante's and Courtney's in that the eighth graders, except for Zoey, intimidated me and I often felt on the outside of the group trying to worm my way in. But unlike Courtney, they always included me in conversations and talked about doing things together.

Elijah's crowd was very different because they liked to laugh and have fun. And I had fun with them. They had their own thing going where they had plenty of power and popularity and didn't need to deal with anyone from Courtney's friend group. They were a diverse mix in a sea of conformity and sameness.

I managed to get Zoey talking about soccer some more and soon enough we were back in our own two-person conversation which allowed me to just keep on talking when the warning bell rang so that I *had* to walk with her to her class in order to finish the conversation. She didn't seem to mind at all, encouraging me to continue by asking me questions and giggling at my not-so-clever jokes.

I successfully walked Zoey to class the next three days, too. Then, on Thursday, I messed up on my timing and for the first time all year, I was tardy to a class.

"Mr. Miller," Ms. Woodson barked from the front of the classroom as I rushed to my desk. "You're late," she announced to all before turning her attention back to the large Promethean screen in the middle of the room.

Several boys snickered and made kissing sounds behind me.

I leaned way over to grab my notebook and pencil out of my backpack, effectively hiding the tell-tale flush of my cheeks and smile.

The paste-eater whispered to me, "I heard you're dating The New Girl. She's an eighth grader." It was hard to tell which sentence held more awe, the one about me dating Zoey or the one about her being an eighth grader.

Once again, people were talking about me. This time, I needed to do better, even if it was none of Paste-Eaters business.

"I just walked her to class," I said, finishing the sentence in my head with *for now*. "Why would people think we're dating?"

"Because you keep walking her to class. That's something boyfriends do."

"Is it?"

Nosy Paste-Eater was brighter than I'd given her credit for. So if I was doing what boyfriends did—or what guys who wanted to be a boyfriend did—then could I take Zoey's friendliness when we walked to be a sign she'd be interested in being my girlfriend?

Paste-Eater continued to watch me with a side-eyed stare as I opened my notebook. "Are you going to walk her to her next class?"

"No. Her next class is literally next door."

She smirked.

I wasn't sure why my response earned a smirk from her or why she said, "You make a cute couple," but since she left me alone after that to pay attention to our teacher and take notes, I was thankful.

Ten minutes later, after our teacher had us all take out our Chromebooks then proceeded to mutter at the Promethean board that refused to do what she wanted it to, a crunched up paper ball nailed my shoulder. I grabbed the paper ball and searched the class to find the culprit. The only other person to throw objects at me was Kayla, and she wouldn't waste her effort on a paper ball that did no damage.

"Open it!" a kid behind me ordered.

Ms. Woodson had her back to the class while she punched at the giant screen, temporarily distracted.

I unfolded the paper and pressed the wrinkled sketch of a stick figure kissing another stick figure. The artist was kind enough to include labels to identify me—the skinny stick figure with the bad haircut—and Zoey, the slightly shorter stick figure in a triangle for a skirt. The unknown artist attempted one realistic detail: Zoey's braids with lavender extensions, though they used a red pencil in the drawing.

I scanned the entire class, not sure who on earth drew it. Kayla and Jeff were too far away, and neither were on joking terms with me, if the drawing was indeed a joke.

Behind me, two boys said, "Sean and Zoey sitting in a tree, K-I-S-S-I-N-G."

"Really?" I asked, arching an eyebrow and shaking my head. Were we in first grade again somehow?

Just then, from my backpack came a quick ding and a buzz. With Ms. Woodson preoccupied, I didn't have to be worried about trying to be sly, so I just grabbed my cell for a quick swipe of the screen. Out of nowhere there it was.

A text from Courtney.

Courtney: its Jamba time! after class. U should come.

Was she for real? After cruelly dismissing me and flat out ignoring me for the last three months, she suddenly texted me when I was interested in someone else? What was with her? She clearly didn't care about me. Maybe she was suddenly interested in me again because I was newsworthy again. I wasn't sure which reason was worse.

Did she really think I was that hung up on her? What self-respecting boy would ignore her ruthless streak and want to have anything to do with her after what she did? I stared at the ludicrous text for the longest five seconds of my life before responding.

Me: No.

I shot off my response with no hesitation. A surge of pride swelled in my chest, much like when I made a game-saving tackle or scored a goal. *Thank you, Courtney Crenshaw, for giving me this chance to stand up to you.* What an unexpected treat.

My cell unexpectedly dinged and vibrated again.

Courtney: come with us. It's been 2 long. lets catch up.

Did she not understand what *No* meant? I tried to imagine what life must be like when one was not accustomed to getting everything they wanted, but just the idea of it filled me with anger.

Me: Delete my number.

I pressed send but then immediately regretted it, wishing I could have said something harsher, realizing I would probably never get a chance to tell her how I really felt about her.

"There! It works!" Ms. Woodson spun back around to face us again. Her expression said "ta-da!"

The extra-large screen behind her now said something about screen sharing and there was a code and below it numbered rectangles.

Unlike her normal act of being the perfect student, Courtney now glared at me with a gnarly Cruella Deville worthy frown. She read my text and this time understood it.

"OK class, in order to share your presentation, you need to keep it open on one tab while using another tab to sign into the screen sharing option."

Ms. Woodson wanted us to present our lab summaries we completed on Google slides through the large Promethean using the code to share our screen onto it. It was some extension already programmed in our Chromebooks, supposedly, but it sure looked to me like I could type in the sharing website and enter the code from any device.

Inspiration struck.

I quickly typed the web address into my phone and sure enough, it welcomed me to the Promethean Screen Sharing app for Ms. Woodson's class and asked for my code. On the big Promethean screen, front and center in our class, my name popped into the first rectangle, along with a box next to it.

"Ah, good job, Mr. Miller," Ms. Woodson said, and she used her finger to check the box next to my name.

I held my breath, not sure what was about to happen, but it could be the biggest blunder of my seventh-grade career. Or it could be evil genius type success.

Ms. Woodson returned to stabbing and muttering at the screen as a couple more classmates' names populated the rectangles below mine.

"Ah," Ms. Woodson said with another triumphant whoop as the screen went dark.

I held my breath as the seconds ticked away.

Then my cell phone's screen popped up on the larger-than-life Promethean board, broadcasting Courtney and my texts for the entire class to see.

The jokers behind me were the first to react with loud, guffawing laughter.

Courtney's screech was loud and shrill. "Ms. Woodson!" she cried out. "Turn it off!"

Gasps and laughter erupted from all over the classroom, but at that moment, only one person in the classroom mattered. From across the classroom, Kayla's gaze met mine.

Not only did she maintain eye contact, but she rewarded my act with a smile. An honest to God Kayla Burns smile!

As if they had been waiting forever to do so, my lips curved into the smile reserved for responding to a legit Kayla Burns smile. The moment would forever remain in my mind as The Smile, with the rest of the class in chaos and Ms. Woodson punching at the screen in frustration, nothing but background to our moment.

Then the screen went dark again.

Ms. Woodson spun back around to face me—and only me—with fire in her eyes.

Uh-oh.

Whatever was about to happen, I would not like it one bit.

I sat up in my plastic seat and awaited my reckoning while Ms. Woodson reined in the class. I swore I saw steam seep from her nostrils like a raging bull. And I was the bullfighter's red, taunting flag. There would be consequences. Never had Ms. Woodson looked so pissed.

From her spot up front, Courtney's bright red cheeks, slumped shoulders, and sulking posture were on display for all to see. Never had I seen her look upset, much less defeated.

"Mr. Miller. Miss Crenshaw. Outside. NOW."

The Promethean screen filled with a Bill Nye science video as I jetted outside, thankful for the escape from prying eyes. Outside, I leaned my back against the wall and waited for easily a minute before Courtney slipped out the door, Ms. Woodson at her heels.

Ms. Woodson didn't close the door, needing to monitor the rest of the class, but she didn't lower her voice, either.

"Sean Miller, I don't have to explain to *you* the *many* things you did wrong here."

It wasn't a question, but the way she continued to stare at me made me respond with a quick, "No."

She sent me another fierce glare with a ferocious silent growl, then she turned on Courtney. "Courtney Crenshaw, you texted during *my class* about ditching another class. Are you kidding me?"

For the first time, Courtney had nothing to say. Her face was still a light red and her eyes glistened like she was fighting off tears.

"When we go back into class, you will surrender your phone to me. You will need to check with the office after school to see if you can pick it up or if your parent needs to."

Courtney's chin sank to her neck, but she nodded and slunk back inside.

Then it was just my teacher and me. All her rage directed at just me. The first pang of regret hit.

"You knew exactly what you were doing."

Another statement I wasn't sure how or if to respond to.

"You were texting during *my class* and you intentionally *disrupted my class* and announced to the entire class you were texting *during my class*."

The disrupting class was not my intention. "I'm sorry—"

"Are you?"

I'd never been the recipient of a teacher's evil-eyed glare before. I was in a world of trouble. The troublemaker was a foreign role for me. I followed my gut.

"Disrupting the class was not my intention. I just wanted Courtney to stop."

My teacher gave me a long hard look. "Well, I think you succeeded. Lunch detention for the rest of this week."

It was my turn to slink back into class like I'd single-handedly lost a big playoff game, but as I walked, the big game became a non-elimination game as I realized it was Thursday, so one lunch detention wasn't horrible.

After I surrendered my phone, the video continued playing, more background noise because most of my classmates talked with someone nearby, many eyes shifting to study my every step as I returned to my seat.

Ms. Woodson took control of the class and announced that lab presentations were postponed until tomorrow. The class cheered, which earned me yet another scowl from my teacher.

Missing lunch on Friday wasn't ideal. It was the best part of my day and prime time to talk with Zoey. But did I regret my public revenge?

Not at all.

Sharing my victory with Kayla made it so worth it.

TIP #20 BE HAPPY

SEVENTH GRADE SURVIVAL GUIDE TIP #20 BE HAPPY

Screams bounced off the lockers as I walked towards the buses, holding hands with Zoey, our arms swinging back and forth like we were walking on the beach, just a couple in the mass of students trooping towards the parking lot. It felt so good to have a girlfriend at my side again, holding my hand, as if it was us against anyone who challenged us.

Zoey talked about her upcoming soccer tournament and plans for spring break, and I hoped to watch one of her games between my games, practice, and vacation.

Not far ahead of us in the crowd, Kayla Burns, dressed in ripped jeans and a trendy off-shoulder tee, strolled with Leticia. They walked with linked elbows, heads bent toward the other, like they whispered highly confidential secrets to each other. It was an odd sight. The seventh-grade version of Shondra, Letty talked trash like the boys on my soccer team and could run as fast as us, too. What did she and Kayla have in common to be so close so suddenly?

It had been three long months since our breakup, and while she no longer stared straight through me—a huge win—we were a long way from being friends again. Our conversation about Tuck, her accepting my apology, and our shared smile during science meant everything to me, and while it meant something to Kayla, too, it hadn't been enough for us to start back talking like friends, which was probably a lot to ask for. But it would have been nice to at least be able to say "Hi," on a regular basis.

After a couple of attempts at conversation on my part, and a couple of tight, tiny smiles and quick disappearances on her part, I learned to accept her small smiles as the best response. At least we no longer had to ignore each other. These little victories, over time, would have to d o.

Lately her clothes and appearance acted like a mood ring, changing as often as I changed the batteries for my Xbox controller. I had no idea what was actually going on with Kayla. She was still close friends with Jeff, but I didn't talk to him. All I knew for sure was the Kayla in front of me now was a different person from the girl I was friends with in September.

That afternoon, Kayla strutted like a cheerleader in her ankle boots, her laughter lingering in her wake like a brilliant rainbow after a storm as she and Leticia marched past all the lines of students waiting to load onto the school buses.

I kissed Zoey on the lips, gave her my best sweet smile, and received her sly grin in return. She waved goodbye before I headed to the last line.

I joined Elijah at the end of the line. An all too familiar rumbling had me glancing at the entrance of the parking lot. It sounded just like Tuck's car.

Sure enough, his Gremlin swerved into the parking lot.

Joy at the sight lifted me out of my funk at this long-awaited sight.

The Gremlin cruised down into the parking lot, screeching to a halt at the curb behind my bus. Queen's Bohemian Rhapsody blasted from the open windows.

How long had it been since I last saw him and his crazy car? A month? Maybe more. Without a word or glance to Elijah, I abandoned my bus line and walked over to Tuck's car like a zombie in one of my games. I brushed right past Kayla, who stood next to the car while giving her friend a hug, acting as oblivious to me as I pretended to be of her.

"Tuck!" I half waved to him as I approached the passenger door and ducked to look inside.

"Hey, LD," he said with a lazy smile.

Too many questions filled my head for me to pick which to ask. He looked like Tuck. Same gold rimmed round glasses, same curly and unruly hair, and same half sardonic, half friendly smile. It could have been my imagination, but his eyes didn't hold the cheer of his tone or the friendliness of his smile.

"Are you OK?" I asked. It wasn't the top question I wanted to ask, but it was the safest one with the best chance of an answer.

"Sure," he said absently. "Sure," he repeated with a little shrug.

I realized Elijah had followed me from the bus line. "You remember Elijah, right?"

Tuck's gaze slid past me to glance at my friend for a second. "Sure. What's up?"

"Hey," Elijah said, his voice quiet. He knew all about Tuck's mysterious disappearance.

"We should go to the beach sometime over break," I said. Elijah almost stifled his groan of disagreement.

But Tuck gave me another smile, this one more carefree than the last one. "Yeah, sure," he said.

A hand clutched my arm like a cuff and firmly pulled me away from the door.

"You're in my way," Kayla said easing past me.

"Oh, sorry," I quickly mumbled and further stepped back for her to open the door. She flung open the passenger door with a loud creak–a well-known noise somehow louder than the Bohemian Rhapsody.

"My ride," she said with a simple shrug.

I wanted to ask why Tuck was picking her up. I wanted to ask why Tuck disappeared and made everyone worry. I wanted to ask a ton more questions, but I knew my time was up.

Elijah made this clear by leaving me to hurry over to our bus. There was no longer a line, and the first bus had already left.

After Kayla slammed the door twice, I leaned over and waved to Tuck. "I gotta go."

He raised his hand in a hint of a wave and said, "See you later, LD."

I didn't want to go, but I had to. "Bye, Tuck. Bye, Kayla." I turned and hurried over to my bus.

Tires squealed behind me and I knew it was Tuck's Gremlin pulling away from the curb. Tuck and Kayla and the car shot past my bus.

Once seated in the back of the bus, Elijah frowned at me some more.

"So we're still going to the beach with him?"

I shrugged. "I have no idea."

Elijah nodded. "At least you and Kayla are talking again."

"Yeah. At least there's that."

TIP #21 JUST BE FRIENDS

When I walked into class that first day back from Spring Break, naturally the first face I recognized was Kayla's–even if her actual face looked nothing like her. She chopped her hair short and added heavy purple streaks throughout. She wore wore a trendy, tight, black t-shirt with ripped jean shorts, striped knee socks and Vans, big silver hoop earrings, big silver hoop earrings, and the biggest shocker: tons of makeup. It could be a skater look, probably not too far from the surfer look, but still, it wasn't Kayla.

She was for some reason seated near my seat, but a quick glance around told me everyone seated was in a new spot.

I raised a hand in a half wave and said, "Hey," in my ultra casual greeting that seemed to be the safest with her.

The corners of her mouth curved up in a legit smile. It was so good to worthy of a Kayla Burns smile again.

"Hey," she said, with a simple head nod.

With a silly grin on my lips, I searched for my assigned seat. According to the seating chart displayed on the Promethean Board, I was now seated in the middle of the entire class—and right next to Jeff Grayson.

Jeff breezed through the door right after I sat down and froze in mid-step, just like everyone else, as he saw all the students in new seats. Unlike Kayla and her small but present smile, when his eyes met mine, a million and one conflicting emotions flashed across his face. He strode through class, said, "Hey, KB," as he passed in front of her desk, and earned a sparkling smile from her, reminding me that they were still friends. Was he rubbing it in my face that he somehow stayed friends with Kayla while I had to work hard just to get a smile from her?

"'Sup," he said to me in a too loud greeting as he tossed his backpack on the desk next to me. He dropped into the seat, his knees splayed wide in his trendy ripped jeans, taking up every inch of his space.

The bell rang. Ms. Woodson directed the stragglers to their seats, and then she launched into a summary of her spring break complete with Google Slides presentation and way too many pictures of her home garden.

Our first assignment: interview our new "elbow partner".

"Dude," Jeff said, rocking his chair back from the desk and angling his body towards me. "How lucky are we?" His casual posture warred with his sarcastic smirk. I couldn't tell which emotion was true. Despite his tone and smirk, did he mean it? Despite the relaxed way he leaned back in his chair, was he worried about how I was going to respond? We hadn't talked or texted, hardly even gamed online, or anything since January when everything with Kayla blew up in my face.

"Yeah. Lucky." The last word tasted wrong with the tone I used. I let out a long sigh. Wasn't I missing his friendship just the other day? Didn't I wish for a way to fix things between us? Did Ms. Woodson have some secret agenda behind this seating assignment? "What's new with you?"

He shrugged, but then grinned. "Not much. Just Jeff as usual."

Except he wasn't "just Jeff." Kayla wasn't the only one who went through a complete makeover. Jeff was easily an inch taller, his shoulders inches broader than mine. Gone was his Dodger's hat and shirt, even though the new season had just started. Along with his stylish jeans, he wore black Chuck Taylor Converse sneakers and a basic Lucky Jeans brand shirt. He even had a sharp haircut with bangs and streaks and stuff.

Perhaps because of my intense inspection, he added, "You know, baseball camp by day, Xbox by night, all break long. You?"

"Soccer tournaments and practice, and Xbox, the usual."

An eyebrow raised. "Who're you playing with now?"

"Mostly Elijah and Antoine, and some of the guys. Sometimes Mitch."

"One minute to wrap it up," our teacher called over the talking.

One minute, just one more minute to resist the temptation of asking the only question I really wanted to know. Why did he throw away our friendship for, what was it, one week with Kayla? But even as I fought the urge to ask him the burning question, another question rose: how was he still friends with her? More questions regarding Kayla flooded my thoughts.

Suddenly, the need to conquer my curiosity evaporated, leaving me with the burning need to ask him all my questions. I just couldn't decide which question to ask first.

"Why did you do it?"

Jeff blinked. "Do what?"

"Date Kayla right after we broke up."

"Dude. How many times do Mitch and I have to tell you? Kayla and I never dated."

I stared at him forever, watching for his tells. He didn't roll his eyes or look away. In fact, he looked more annoyed with me with each second. "Mitch never said that. And you and her were holding hands—a lot."

Jeff cursed. "Mitch was supposed to tell you. I tried to tell you. We never dated, we never called each other, we never did anything like that."

"But you were so close."

"Dude. You screwed up. You were stupid and she didn't deserve it."

I wanted to argue that as my friend, he should have taken my side, but I couldn't, because I know it wasn't true. I had screwed up. Once again, I was the bad guy and Kayla didn't deserve it. Jeff was right. He protected a friend.

"OK," our teacher said in a loud, commanding voice, preventing me from saying more to Jeff. "Each partner group will stand and share one thing you learned about your new elbow partner."

Oh happy day, we got to stand and share in front of the entire class.

Kayla's partner shared that Kayla's new passion in life was running track and that she won second place in her first meet. I wished she would have elaborated or given us a chance for questions. Kayla was a runner? This was news to me. Also, I didn't know there were track teams for middle school students. Why hadn't I heard of it? Not that I had time for another sport, I barely had time to squeeze baseball into my schedule with so much time dedicated to my soccer team.

I remembered Letty and Kayla walking together like the best of friends before break and one piece to the puzzle of New Kayla fell into place. Letty was one of the fastest sprinters in school. If Kayla was now running sprints for this mysterious track team, she must surely run with Letty.

Kayla provided a ton of descriptive detail on her partner's spring break trip to Mexico.

Too soon, it was our turn. Jeff and I stood.

I cleared my throat. "This is Jeff Grayson." After this, I stalled. We hadn't really talked about anything–nothing worth sharing with the class. It wasn't like I learned anything new that I could share with the class. That he and Kayla hadn't dated wasn't something to share with the class. "He has two older brothers." Stick with the facts, right? But that boring fact wasn't really being fair to Jeff. "He's big into baseball–his favorite team is the Dodgers. He's a star first baseman and a classic cleanup hitter."

Jeff quickly and casually rattled off my information. "Sean Miller, everyone. He plays a ton of soccer, gets straight A's, and still has time for Xbox marathons in his free time."

In the beginning of the year, Jeff telling the class I was a smart straight-A student would have horrified me as I tried so hard to play down my academic achievements. Now, I beamed with pride. Yes, I was smart and athletic, and I was proud to be both. I wondered how Jeff knew I had changed, because he never would have busted me out like that when I was downplaying my grades.

Together, Jeff and I sat.

While Kayla and my friendship ended in an explosion of emotions, and Courtney and my fake friendship ended with cold, calculated actions, Jeff and my long-time friendship sank like the Titanic in three distinct stages.

The initial impact: consoling Kayla and holding her hand after she attacked me in class.

The damage: taking my place by walking her to her next class. Even worse, he walked her from their last class to her locker that day, and I swear they held hands while doing so.

The sinking: Effectively replacing me in Kayla's life as her best guy friend, even if they never actually dated.

Sitting next to him many months later, with much of the sting of his believed betrayal dulled, with him sneaking sly smiles and whispering funny comments under his breath, it reminded me of how much I liked science class when Jeff and I were friends. Could it be that easy? Could we pick up where we left off in December of last year, pretend like January didn't happen, and be friends again?

During the next pair-share activity, when we were supposed to discuss our semester goals, I instead asked him, "Have you played the new season of Smash Rocket Racers?"

He responded with his classic cocky grin that promised me anything was possible. "Of course. I'm crushing it."

We launched into an animated update of all our Xbox pursuits. Each time Jeff grinned or laughed, I felt a little lighter, and a little happier. I missed my friend. If Kayla could forgive me for the horrible way I behaved, I should forgive Jeff for taking her side in the breakup. He was the true friend in the scenario, supporting the one who needed it the most and who was the innocent victim. I needed to be more like Jeff.

I was ready to be a good friend again. "What are we playing tonight?"

WANT TO READ MORE?

Sneak-peak: Book 2

How to Survive a Breakup Chapter 1

THE LITTLE BELLS JINGLED joyfully from earlobes as I walked hand in hand with my boyfriend through the halls of our middle school. Big lightbulbs flashed from my holiday sweater that I would never call ugly. It was the last day before Christmas break and my festive outfit helped deck our school halls, which was a wide, main paved path of blacktop connecting large courtyards protected the east side of campus by two-story buildings .

"Kayla! Sean!" Thea rushed over to us with a smile about to bust open her face. "I did it! I won first chair!"

I squealed, she squealed, we both squealed, loud and joyous, neither caring who thought what about our squeals. Then the hugging began.

"Of course, you got it. Congratulations, Thea!" I said, my smile as ecstatic hers. "I knew you would do it. I'm so proud of you."

Whatever Thea wanted, Thea got. Not by asking for it like one of the many spoiled rich kids at our school, but by working her butt off to achieve it. She was my IRL hero.

While she wasn't as decked out as I was for the holidays, she reminded me of Rudolph the Reindeer in her brown sweater, tan corduroy pants, and antler head band that had flashing red lights. Just behind each antler, her panda buns poofed out in perfect symmetry.

"Yeah, congratulations, Thea," Sean said. "You deserve it."

My boyfriend was so cute, standing next to me, still holding my hand, being so nice to my bestie. Unlike Thea and me, my boyfriend of two months and ten days (and counting!) wore nothing that suggested he celebrated Christmas, like he somehow forgot that it was a few days before Christmas.

"Are you and your family going out to celebrate?" I asked Thea.

"Maybe." She shrugged, but her smile conveyed the pride and excitement she tried to downplay. She veered off to the right, waving a hand behind her. "One class to go! See you after school!"

Sean walked with me to my last class. It was so cool of him to walk me to class, even though it was in the opposite direction of his class. In fact, thanks to celebrating with Thea, he'd have to jam across campus to avoid being tardy.

"Thea is amazing." I couldn't think of a time when she wasn't victorious. "I'm so proud of her."

"Yeah." Sean looped his thumbs under his backpack straps, an action he did often during our walk to class.

"What about you?" I asked him. "Any big soccer games or tournaments over break?" I took a quick breath and rushed through my next question before doubt stopped me. "Maybe I can go to a game to cheer for you?"

"No," he said.

And that's why I had doubts. I had never asked about watching him play before, mainly because I saw him enough at school, but the thought of not seeing him for two and a half weeks made me desperate to see him.

Before the sting from his quick rejection could really set in, he continued with a reassuring smile. "We get the entire break off."

Relief washed through me, calming the flush from his initial rejection. No soccer for two and a half weeks was a big deal in his world of competitive soccer because he practiced three times a week and had at least one game each weekend.

My pride restored, a teasing spirit guided me through my next words. "So you will have some time to just be a kid and play Xbox?"

His green eyes lit up. "Yes. Nothing but Xbox and surfing and maybe some snowboarding."

We stopped off to the side when we reached my classroom, letting classmates flow by us. We shared a quick peck on the lips. Then he waved, did a quick pivot maneuver in his soccer style Adidas sneakers, and was off, heading back to the main part of school and his last class.

As I watched him go, I caught sight of Courtney Crenshaw and her minions stalking towards him with matching, determined sneers. Courtney gave him her tinkling fingers wave, which never failed to hook him. He waved back, and I didn't need to see his face to see that dopey smile he reserved just for her—his "it's my lucky day because Courtney acknowledged me" ecstatic smile. At least this time he kept walking towards class, which left Courtney and her friends to pretend that was their plan all alone, just to wave to him in passing.

For the millionth time, I wondered how I got so lucky to have Sean Miller as my boyfriend. He was so cute and so smart and so fun to be around. And until I kissed him at the dance, I thankfully had no competition. It was only after the kiss when Courtney noticed him. But she was too late. He was mine.

Vowing to forget about Courtney's existence, I darted into my classroom seconds before the bell rang. I loved ending school with my favorite subject. My table of four was up front, where I sat next to a quiet girl and across from a loud boy and a silly boy. It wasn't who I would sit with if I had the choice, but it worked OK.

My English teacher greeted us seconds after the bell rang.

"Welcome class," she said, not in a tired way, nor in a pumped up way, more matter-of-fact, as if it weren't the last period before two and a half weeks off! "Many of you still need to finish your argumentative essay. Today's the last day of the quarter. Turn them in already." She preceded to list all the students who still needed to turn in their essay. I finished mine two days ago. I finished all assignments in all my classes by Wednesday. So as soon as she released us to work independently, I pulled out my Chromebook and brought up my blog.

It was more a combo blog and vlog, sometimes I posted long, clever rants or raves about something that amused or upset me; other times I posted video diaries on whatever moved me at the moment. Today I wanted to rave about how awesome the last day of school before a long break was.

The Last Class of the Year!

After months of anticipation, Christmas break is finally here! And the last day of school is ending with a bang.

> 1. *My bestie just won first chair in the orchestra. She's been practicing, and even has a private coach, so she more than deserves it.*

> 2. *My boyfriend's soccer team is in first place for their region and his team won break from soccer, which is perfect for him since*

he's spending half his break surfing in Hawaii.

3. *My other bestie...*

My partner next to me pounded away at her keyboard with a punch-punch-punch, doing the hunt and peck method while my fingertips flew across the keyboard like it was a piano. Sometimes I swore I heard music coming from my movements.

Like when I was reading a good book, I lost myself in my blogging, where everyone and everything else in the classroom disappeared, as if I was alone in an empty room. I sped through my re-read and was almost done with the fifth paragraph when suddenly a sharp object poked me in the rib.

I jumped in my seat. "Ouch!"

Vicki flashed me a small but sly grin.

"What was that for?" I rubbed my rib, as if that would help relieve the dull ache.

Vicki's smile widened, unashamed. "How do you spell courage?"

"Courage? C-o-u-r-a-g-e. Like rage, but with a c-o-u in front."

Huh. Funny to share similar word parts, courage and rage, but have two very different meanings. The English language was funny like that. I couldn't think of a way to incorporate this new thought into my blog and soon it was but a distant memory as my typing blended in with the rest of the class.

While my boyfriend surfs in Hawaii and my besties spend time with their families, my friend Jeff is going skiing in Mammoth. People who don't live in Southern California think we live 24-7 in sundresses and swimsuits. Not true. What is true is that we can surf in the morning and snowboard in the afternoon, but the snow will probably be slushy.

Another pencil jab into the ribs.

This time I leaned far away from her. "Stop that."

"How do you spell bravery?"

"Can't you use spell check?" I risked looking at her Chromebook screen, which meant leaning a little too close to the stabber. Typed on her screen was *b-r-e-w-y*. No, spell check wouldn't know what to do with that. "B-r-a-v-e-r-y."

Vicki didn't thank me, but she typed the letters I told her to, so I guess that was her thank you. Both words she asked me how to spell were in our notes, but I did my best not to be snotty to others in class.

The silly boy across from us rudely snickered. He was not above being snotty. "How do you not know how to spell bravery and courage?"

As was my MO, I struck back as if he had insulted me and not the girl who kept stabbing me with her pencil. "Who are you to judge? Your essay is half a page. At least her essay is over a page."

The boy's face contorted into an ugly sneer. "My essay's a page."

My eyes narrowed. The silly boy hadn't annoyed me like this before. Didn't he realize I detested liars as much as I hated bullies? "At 18-point font. When Mrs. Parker reduces the font to 12-point, it's going to shrink to-" and I held up my hand with my pointer finger hovering just above my thumb, "-half a page."

"What?" he sputtered. "Why are you just telling me now?" He glared at me as if I was responsible for his schoolwork.

Once our conversation moved away from her spelling, Vicki returned to typing and it appeared unlikely she would return the favor by defending me.

I sighed, wishing I could be a little snotty and tell the boy I didn't have to help him at all. "If you un-submit it in Google Classroom, you can fix the font and you'll see."

He let out a louder sigh, but soon enough, he joined the merry melody of typing.

Desperate to reenter my writer zone, I slipped on earbuds and keyed up my pop Christmas songs playlist on Spotify.

Seconds later, or maybe minutes, as I added several more paragraphs to my blog, the bell rang.

School was out for eighteen days!

I hit the publish button on my blog, tucked my Chromebook back in its pouch in my backpack, and grabbed my jacket from the chair. I followed the mass of students rushing the door to escape, joining in with everyone else shouting, "See you next year!"

Bursting outside, the gray sky reminded me it was a blistery chilly afternoon. I pulled on my puffy jacket, then wrapped it tighter so that it overlapped in front. As one of the crowd of sixth, seventh and eighth graders streaming towards the front of school, I followed the flow, keeping an eye out for Sean. Even though we talked before my last class, I really wanted to see him one more time before the long break.

Unfortunately, the entire school flooded the halls, filling the "hallways" with bundled up bodies mixed with a couple students in t-shirts and shorts. That morning my app told me it was 60 degrees with little hope of it getting any warmer. Why people were wearing t-shirts and shorts? No idea.

I rode the tide all the way to the entrance of the school where I veered sharply to the left with half the students. A line of five yellow school buses waited in front of the school. Mine was always one of the last ones in line, so I headed to the back bus. Sean's bus was, as usual, a couple ahead of mine.

I found him and his best friend Jeff towards the front of their line, about to board. I rushed over and tapped Sean's arm.

"Merry Christmas, Sean," I said with a shy smile, and before I could think better of it, gave his cheek a quick kiss. I earned a sweet smile from him.

Then I stepped back with a small wave as both boys smiled and waved to me before they stepped up onto the bus.

Saturday morning, three days before Christmas, Dad and I were halfway through our annual Dad and Daughter Bake-off when Mom sat down at the counter with her laptop and a coffee.

"Mmmmm," Mom said. She took a sip of coffee before added, "Smells like Christmas."

"It's another Burns Christmas in the making," Dad said, tapping his Darth Vader apron, the one that light up with red lights and when pressed, said *Luke, I am your father*.

I pushed my sleeves up past my elbows, adjust the straps of my Wonder Woman apron around, and said, "Alexa, play the top Christmas songs."

Seconds later Mariah Carey's *All I want for Christmas* song started playing in the family room.

"Now it smells *and* sounds like Christmas."

By the time my older sister joined the living, the delightful vanilla and cinnamon aroma of freshly baked goods filled the kitchen. The cake, rolled into a log and cooling to be frosted, sat on the countertop with the neatly stacked cookies in containers on one side, and the braided bread cooling on the rack on the other side, its golden crust yeasty and tempting.

"The whole house stinks."

My older sister shuffled into the kitchen, only one eye cracked open and her hair a rat's nest. Leave it to Alicia to be disgusted by the delicious smells of a bakery right in her own home.

"Are you feeling OK?" Mom asked Alicia.

Alicia combed her fingers through her tangled hair, grimacing as she yanked and pulled. "I'm fine," she muttered.

I couldn't remember a time when she looked less fine. Why would she lie about how she felt? Was it so hard to be honest? "Do you want a Snickerdoodle cookie?" I asked, hoped it would cheer her up. "They're delicious."

But Alicia spun around and stomped out of the kitchen and back down the hallway to her room.

Soon enough Alicia and her odd behavior were a distant memory as I ran around the house tiding up as best I could before our family arrived later that day. Then it was on to cleaning my bedroom. I tidied up the shelves that house all my prize collections, like my shell collection and my Lego Wonder Woman and her Invisible Jet.

Exhausted after all my cleaning, I grabbed my phone and collapsed on my bed. I wanted to call Sean. He was leaving for Hawaii later that day. I couldn't imagine spending Christmas surrounded by sand and palm trees, but it was his family's Christmas tradition and he insisted it was perfect.

I wanted nothing more than to talk to him for the next hour, but my gut told me to wait. Why? He was my boyfriend. I could call him whenever I wanted, right? We'd been dating for close to three months. Wasn't it better to call him now instead of when he was in Hawaii?

I called him.

He answered after the third ring. "Hi Kayla. What's up?"

"Nothing much. I just finished cleaning the house and now I'm waiting for family to show up. I thought I'd call and wish you a good flight."

"Oh, thanks. Yeah, just finished packing."

"When do you leave?"

"Any minute now."

"I've never been to Hawaii. You'll take some pictures, right?"

"Yes. I have an underwater camera we use when we go snorkeling. I might try to get some pictures while surfing."

"Oh wow. Will you be able to capture some of your trick moves?" He started going to surf camp when he was nine, so he had been doing it for a couple of years more than me, and was a great surfer.

"Yeah, I think so."

During the lull in our conversation, I could hear my sister's voice through our shared bedroom wall. Her voice continued to get louder and less muffled, like she was arguing with someone–and the someone wasn't a mystery.

"Alicia and Tuck are *not fighting* again," I told Sean.

"Again? They seem to do that a lot lately."

"Yeah." I sighed. My sister and her boyfriend's "not fighting" was becoming a problem. They had only been dating a couple weeks more than Sean and me, but they were seniors in high school and apparently had a lot more to disagree about.

"Well, I gotta go. In case we don't get a chance to talk, Merry Christmas, Kay."

"Merry Christmas, Sean! Have a great trip."

After hanging up with Sean, I hugged myself, enjoying the warm and cozy feeling. I was the luckiest girl in the world to have him as my boyfriend.

Acknowledgements

This book would not exist for your reading enjoyment if it weren't for many people. My editor, Tami Jeffers, and my cover designer, Suzanna with Elefont Books, were instrumental in the creation process for a professional book. My writing partners, Emily, Lynn, and Pam, are essential components to my writing process. I wouldn't be able to spend hours a day writing away if I didn't have full support from my family. My dad and aunt are my biggest cheerleaders. Also, my beta readers, Jill, Lynn, my aunt Janie, and my son Thomas, all played crucial parts in the revision process. My other son, Joseph, read enough to engage in a dinner table discussion about Sean—never did I envision my family discussing one of my characters like he was a real person. It was truly a *you-know-you're-a-real-writer-when* moment. Finally, I am so grateful for all the wonderful writers I met at the 20Books Vegas 2023 convention, and especially those who were on my Author Series podcast. Your advice, support, and encouragement carried me through the many challenges of publishing.

About the Author

HEATHER LIVES, WORKS, AND plays in the San Francisco Bay Area. She is the debut author of the young adult book *Sean's Survival Guide, Book 1* of the Surviving Seventh Grade series. She earned her Master of Fine Arts in Writing from Lindenwood University and has taught English and history in middle school since 2016. Her twin sons graduated from high school and will be off to college soon, but she hopes her two standard poodles, Kirby and Chewy, will be with her for a very long time.